FAUXMANCES & WEDDING BOUQUETS

A SERENADE CREEK NOVEL

ALWAYS A BRIDESMAID
BOOK 1

NATALIE MAY

CONTENTS

IMPORTANT BOUQUET-RELATED DISCLAIMERS

From Bailey, perpetual bouquet catcher:

Hey there, readers! Just a heads-up before you dive in—so that you know what to expect from my love story.

This is a kisses-only romance. No graphic scenes, no profanity, no drug use, and one small polite sip of champagne (nothing wild—I promise). Just awkward flirting, fake dating, and a whole lot of feelings I did not sign up for.

Oh, and about that wedding? The bride (Jessa) is already pregnant when the book starts. She and her longtime love, Luke, have been together for fourteen years, and had intended to be married years ago...before the pregnancy. Needless to say, this wedding means the world to her. Which is how I ended up in a borrowed dress, in a shared suite, fake-dating my boss. Horrible idea by the way.

So if you're looking for a clean, wholesome story with heart, humor, and a sprinkle of small-town chaos... welcome to Serenade Creek. Just don't stand too close to the bouquet. Trust me on that one.

CHAPTER ONE

If a Michaels and a Chuck E. Cheese got into a fight, the aftermath might still look tidier than my classroom. I was surrounded by glitter, cheese cracker crumbs, and townwide murmurs that I might be unlovable... so, you know, just another Friday.

It was the last day of school before summer, and while the rest of the faculty had gone into celebration mode hours ago, I—like the crayons melting on the windowsill—felt worn down to a stub. Too exhausted to even whisper, *Yay*.

While I should've been thinking about restoring some semblance of order within these four walls, I was thinking about the wedding last weekend. That stupid bouquet. And how the so-called love magic of Serenade Creek had it out for me.

The clock, which had matched my vibe and gone into slow-mo mode, finally dragged itself to 1:45.

I clapped my hands.

"Everybody, please line up and head back quietly to Mrs. Dalton's room for your end-of-the-year party. Have a great—"

I'd planted the sugary dream-about-to-come-true of cupcakes and cookies into twenty-five little prefrontal cortexes and the resulting chaos cut off the rest of my half-hearted sentiment.

There would be no lining up today. No quiet. No point in trying to rein in what I'd unleashed.

"See you in the fall!" I called, as they stampeded out the door. I could only hope there was no one in the hallway for them to bum rush. "Have a good—"

"Miss Cooper! Miss Cooper!" Avalynn, the tiniest and most mature second grader I'd ever had the pleasure of teaching, came racing back. She flung herself at me, wrapping her arms around my thighs in what I like to call a cub hug.

After a valiant attempt at cutting off the circulation in my lower body, she pulled away and looked up at me. Tears spilled out of the corners of her huge brown eyes, rolling down her cheeks.

"Oh, Avalynn. I'm going to miss you, too, sweetheart!" I said, getting a surge of *THIS IS WHY I DO THIS!* in my veins.

Moments like this make it all worth it.

Her bottom lip quivered. She scrunched up her eyes. Then she wailed, "It's just so sad that you're dying!"

And that doesn't even crack the top ten list of startling things children have said to me this week.

"Aww, honey." I kneeled down so I was on her level and

put a reassuring hand on her shoulder as sobs racked her body. "I am not dying."

Unless you know something I don't.

But it isn't appropriate to ask an eight-year-old if they're a clairvoyant...

Her sobs melted into hiccups, then sniffles. I grabbed a tissue off my desk for her inevitably runny nose. I love kids, I do, but they are just little bodily function factories, aren't they?

Opening her eyes, she stared at me with far too much skepticism for someone who hadn't even been on this planet a decade.

"That's not what Gramma Peach said." She straightened her shoulders and put her fists on her hips, and leaned forward in a way that told me she'd seen someone else assume that pose before, probably accompanied with the words *Do not lie to me!* "Gramma Peach told Daddy you're going to die alone like Great Auntie Clara did!"

Ah.

So the grown-up gossip had trickled alllllllll the way down to, well, here and now.

I sighed and stood, imagining the message I'd send to my friends' group chat later:

Welp, I won't be joining you at the Gather & Grill tonight. Going to get Spinster tattooed on my forehead instead.

"Avalynn," I told her in the gentlest voice I could muster. "Honey. I promise you. That will be a long time from now."

"Five years?"

"More than that."

"Ten years?"

"More than that."

Her eyes went wide. "Millions of years?" she whispered.

"Somewhere between ten years and a million, yes. Now, you're missing—"

"Gramma Peach said you're cursed because of the internal bouquet," she went on.

Do not dramatically roll your eyes or pantomime fainting in front of a student, Bailey Cooper.

From the doorway, someone cleared their throat.

I glanced up to see Jocelyn Stillwell, the music teacher, with her eyebrows halfway to heaven.

"You need to go on to Ms. Dalton's room," I told Avalynn.

"Yes, but—"

"No, buts. If you miss last dismissal, you technically have to stay here with me all summer, you know," I nodded like it was a fact.

"All summer!" she cried and, my imminent demise forgotten, hightailed it out.

"The kids have heard about the Eternal Bouquet debacle, huh?" Jocelyn asked, her voice and eyes filled with pity.

My lips parted to say I didn't know if it qualified as a debacle, but then I immediately shut my mouth, because let's be honest: In this town? It does.

The Eternal Bouquet isn't just a bunch of wilting roses held together with luck and floral wire. It's a legend. An actual artifact, passed from bride to bride at every wedding in Serenade Creek since 1982. And when it's tossed at the reception? The single woman who catches it will meet "The One" and be engaged within the year.

And until me, it had a perfect record.

Until me.

I've caught it five times.

The first time, people were thrilled for me. The second time, they were amused. The third time, it got weird. By the fourth, concerned whispers started. As of last weekend and unlucky number five, I'm the woman who broke the bouquet. The harbinger of failed fate. Miss Havisham with glitter in her hair.

"Bailey?" Jocelyn prompted.

I rubbed my face like I could wipe away the past two minutes. "Yes? What can I do for you, Jocelyn?"

Her eyes lit up.

Dang it.

Can't I just say, 'How are you doing?' like a normal human and not address everyone like I'm their employee?

"Ooooh, I am so glad you asked. Well, it's not something you can do for me, per se. But Hammy doesn't have a home for the summer yet. Mrs. Wyatt is asking us all, but I thought... didn't Bailey keep him last year? And since she knows his routine, wouldn't she be the best candidate for the job?"

Hammy. Hammy the Hamster. The school's mascot.

"Um, well—"

"Also, how many pies can I put you down for, hon?"

"I wasn't going to do Piepalooza this year—"

Jocelyn gasped theatrically. "Bailey Cooper! Of course you are!"

"Jocelyn—"

"Pecan, obviously. Five'll do, seven would be better. Bless you."

"I really don't..." My voice trailed off. Jocelyn was not listening. She was *scribble, scribbling* on her emotional support clipboard. Negotiation over.

"And don't forget Hammy!" she called over her shoulder as she breezed out.

I stared after her.

I seriously considered hiding in the supply closet until September, but instead slumped to the floor, one unpaid favor away from being declared a town utility.

A jar of contraband fluffy slime—pink, sparkly, and sans lid—had rolled under the edge of the table closest to me. I grabbed it and scooped some out. It was still soft and airy. I made a fist and squished it in my palm absentmindedly.

Movement at the window caught my eye. The cardinal that had been hanging around was perched on the window ledge, staring in. Head tilted. Eyes bright. And maybe a little judgey.

"I don't know what's wrong with me, so don't even ask," I told him.

I don't know how long I sat there, playing with the slime, but I might have stayed all summer if the door hadn't creaked open behind me startling me out of my stupor.

"Do I even want to know what happened in here?" a deep voice I'd know anywhere asked. "Or should I just go ahead and alert FEMA?"

I twisted, looking over my shoulder and my heartbeat sped up considerably.

Knox Showalter stood there, all 6'3" of him, with that dark hair, those ridiculously blue eyes, and freckles that made his fair skin look like a perfectly painted canvas.

To prevent myself from letting out a dreamy sigh, I pressed my lips together, then made the corners go up in something that might look like a smile if he was very, very nearsighted.

As gracefully as possible, I got to my feet.

Knox tilted his head and looked me over. I mean... he didn't look me over like... you know, he's a man and I'm a woman he finds attractive. He looked me over like he's the assistant principal of Serenade Creek Elementary and I'm one of his staff members who may be on the verge of a mental breakdown.

"How ya doin', Bailey?" he asked.

"Erm." My brain short-circuited at the way he said my name. Low, careful, like it mattered. Like I mattered. It wasn't just that he was hot. It was that he made you feel like if everything went sideways, he'd be the guy who still had a working flashlight and a spare granola bar.

He nudged the door closed behind him and let me tell you... the dreams I have had that started out like this...

He shoved his hands in the pockets of his perfectly pressed khakis which he wore with a lilac button-down—how does he get through an entire day with nary a wrinkle?—and a coordinating polka dot tie that had probably never seen a stain.

We won't even talk about my outfit, but I had dried snot on my sleeve. Someone else's snot, to be clear.

"I'm great!" I chirped. Telling people what they want to hear is kind of my jam.

"Mm-hmm," he said, glancing around. Then he began singing the chorus of that old Rockwell song, "Somebody's Watching Me".

First: My word, does this man have a voice. Second: Oh my gosh. Was that his not-so-subtle way of calling out my tendency to accidentally ogle him?

Before I could roll downhill into a complete panic, he pointed and said, "I like the googly eyes."

I looked around. Googly eyes, from pebble-sized to full-on ones that could be used as teacup saucers, were stuck to everything. The stapler, the trashcan, the rim of my coffee mug. Probably my soul.

"Oh. Oh." And because, hey, the more the merrier: "Oh."

I started moving, picking up this, that, and the other, because this place was a disaster.

"I'm sorry it's such a mess," I said, righting a chair that had somehow been... wronged. "You're not here to fire me for ushering in a construction paper blizzard on school grounds, are you?"

He laughed. "I am not."

Trying not to think about how much I loved his laugh, I scurried over to the markers. I needed to test them and toss the ones that were too dried out to make it to September and make sure the caps were tightly on the good ones. I spent way too much out of my own pocket on supplies this year.

"I let the third graders decorate the classroom with googly eyes," I admitted. "Technically, I was supposed to do papier-mâché with them, but I lacked the will and the budget. Not a criticism of you, by the way—"

"I don't make the budget, Bailey."

Our eyes met. He smiled, sheepish. I felt it in my knees.

He cleared his throat. "So, ah, most of the teachers sprinted out twenty minutes ago. You're the last one here."

I rolled my eyes. Flicking a speck of paint off my jeans, I joked, "You're saying some of us still have the energy to sprint?" I shook my head. "I still have a lot to do. Besides, I like it in here. The last time I went out there, I agreed to the first week of morning car line duty... next year. If I walk out that door, someone else is going to ask me for something.

And I have absolutely nothing left to give. Oh, man. You're not here to ask me for something, are you?"

His expression changed. It wasn't pity, but... concern, maybe.

That was Knox. Level-headed, always calm, the human embodiment of a straight line when the rest of the world was a spiral. He was solid.

"You know it's okay to say no, right?" he asked, gently. "You don't owe everyone your time."

I shrugged. "I think I'm allergic to 'no.' I think about saying no and I break out in hives."

His serious gaze didn't waver, even though I was laughing awkwardly at my own non-joke.

"You give a lot," he said, voice low. "To everyone."

A pause. Too long for comfort.

"Just... don't forget to save a little for yourself."

His gaze darted away like he hadn't meant to say that out loud. I looked down like I hadn't noticed that didn't sound like the assistant principal talking.

That sounded like the guy I met last June who...

I shook my head, to clear it of that thought.

He bent down and scooped up a couple of paint brushes off the floor. Helping me without being asked. It was like watching close-up magic. Swoooon.

"You do not have to do that. And I'm sorry there's glitter on the carpet," I said.

"Would it really be your classroom if it wasn't a little sparkly?" he asked. Then he looked away. Cleared his throat. "So, we missed you at the final assembly."

We? Who was we? Him and... his heart?

"Yeah," I said, trying not to sound too tortured about

missing it, but Knox's weekly assemblies are epic. "Line dancing with the cafeteria ladies, huh?"

"It was pretty awesome." He did a grapevine over to the acrylics, tipped an imaginary hat, and ended with jazz hands.

Suddenly very aware of my own heartbeat, I bit my lip so I wouldn't ask him if he could not be so effortlessly adorable. "I liked your morning announcement, though."

"Thanks. I only bring out my Kermit voice on the most special of occasions." He began straightening toppled bottles. "Why does red always get the glory when magenta is the true primary color? I've always wondered that."

Before I could make up my mind whether he really wanted an explanation or was making small talk, he spoke again.

"So..." he began. "A little birdie told me you missed the assembly because there was some kind of conflict between you and Ms. Machi?"

Margie Machi has been teaching longer than most of the rest of us have been alive and she tends to wield her seniority like a slingshot. And today it was aimed at me. A direct hit.

"You want to tell me what happened?" Knox prodded.

"It's not a big deal," I said. "I was supposed to make posters for the summer STEM program." Because I got voluntold. "And, I got a little overextended." As is my norm. "So I had some fifth and sixth graders help me do it as an extra credit project." Which they were super excited about. "Margie, ah, Ms. Machi wasn't pleased with the result." Even though they were darling and creative as heck. "So I redid them during the assembly."

Also? The windbag told me that I shouldn't use my students as an unpaid labor force, which I really resented.

"Hmm," Knox said. "And it wasn't a big deal?"

I shook my head.

He turned to me, shoved his hands back in his pockets, and watched me, tilting his head one way, then the other.

"You know if anything is troubling you, you can come to me, right?"

I nodded. But... when he said anything, he did not mean *anything*.

I will remain professional.

"I actually was going to touch base with you before the incident with Ms. Machi. Someone said you were a little, erm, emotional in the teachers' lounge this morning."

I cringed.

At least he gave me the grace of not using the phrase *ugly crying*.

"Well," I mumbled. "It's a bittersweet time. End of the year and—"

"Oh. Okay. If that's all." He hesitated. "But I could see how it would be upsetting if even the students have been hassling you about the thing with the, uh, Eternal Bouquet?"

My stomach dropped.

He's heard about it. I'd been hoping since Knox had only been living in Serenade Creek a year, he might not yet be familiar with all of our l'il slice of quaint paradise's eccentricities.

"It must truly look like I just let them run amok in here," I said, as lightly as possible, changing the subject while I rearranged my hair to cover my red-hot ears. Head down, I slipped by him to snatch up a bottle of overturned white glue.

"I didn't stop by to judge, Bailey. I wanted to make sure you were okay."

"I am."

"Okay. Well. I've got a meeting in half an hour so..."

"I guess I'll see you around town this summer," I meant it casually but... Oh, please, oh, please don't let that have come out as *Should I make reservations at The Ampersand for dinner or lunch?*

There was silence that stretched for a beat too long. Long enough for hope to curl up and die politely in the corner.

Finally, Knox shook his head. "Probably not much."

I swallowed hard.

Oh. Right. Okay. Sure.

Then he went on:

"I'll be here for another week or so..." He sighed. Deeply. Like... whatever he was going to be doing in that week, he did not want to be. Wait. Was he leaving? "Then I'm going to be away for most of the break."

He hesitated just long enough to make it feel like he was going to give me more, but then: "Have a good summer, Bailey."

He nodded and smiled and strode to the door, which clicked shut after him.

And then I was alone again.

Well, except for the cardinal that had its beak pressed against the glass and was looking at me like, *Do you think he's going out of town for the break because of what happened at last year's Summer Lovin' Festival, Bailey?*

"No, I do not think that," I said. "That week didn't mean anything to him. That man is not haunted by the Ghost of Summer Flings Past. He's probably just... got fun things planned elsewhere."

I sighed, thinking of my planner for June, July, and

August, jam-packed with everything but fun and anywhere else I'd want to be.

And I mentally penciled in Piepalooza with a sigh.

Maybe this was why the Eternal Bouquet didn't work for me. Because everyone always thought of me when they needed a favor. But I wasn't sure anyone actually saw me as anything other than the helping hand, the always available Bailey Cooper, AKA She Who Always Says Sure, I Can!

CHAPTER TWO

The trick to surviving dining out alone in Serenade Creek was simple: keep your back to the room, keep your mouth full of food, and your answers vague enough that they couldn't be used against you later. Most importantly? Don't let anyone catch a whiff of loneliness on you. No matter how sad you might be, don't you dare look it.

I eat too fast. Always have. But in Serenade Creek, that's a superpower—less downtime between bites, better odds of escaping before any interrogation starts.

Unfortunately, my usual booth at the Gather & Grill—back corner, dim lighting, straight shot to the exits—had been hijacked. The culprits? Retired romantics Ruby, Iris, Cornelia, and Stanley, who liked to call themselves The Cupids, but were more often than not known as the Hearts & Charts Brigade. Which meant I was stuck three booths over, out in the wide open, utterly exposed, while they openly debated the best way to trick me into love.

Iris, with her ever-present crocheted shawl, and Ruby, with her signature stop sign red lipstick and matching scarf, sized me up the same way they had the first time I met them. I shifted in my seat.

Iris clucked her tongue and shook her head. "Still single. Still stubborn. Still a waste of a perfectly fine jawline."

"Perfectly fine is right," Ruby said, waggling her eyebrows at me like I was listed on the menu as the Friday night special.

"Ladies, with all due respect, you're old enough to be my mother—"

Ruby cackled. "Flatterer. I'm old enough to be your grandmother and not a day shy. Besides, I'm happily married as everyone ought to be!"

"Of course, we don't want you for ourselves, Knoxwell," Iris said sweetly. "But if you'd only let us—"

"It's just Knox, Iris," I reminded her.

"You're back at the top of the spreadsheet, you know," Cornelia said, wagging a finger at me. "If you give us a little bit of cooperation, I could point you in the direction of your soul mate in five minutes flat."

"So I could run the other direction in six?" I joked, trying to keep my tone light and inoffensive.

"Nothing wrong with letting 'em chase ya," Stanley said, with a wink. He tipped his glass of tea at me.

Ruby swatted at him. "We will kick you out of this club again if we have to, Stanley."

"Enjoy your dinner," I told them with a polite but hopefully dismissive smile.

Then I took a big swig of my ice water and opened the novel I'd brought along. I actually enjoy reading. It wasn't just a prop to dissuade people from approaching me. Those kinds of social cues don't work in this town.

I'd read three pages when I felt the creeping sensation of someone's gaze on me.

Prepare for interruption in three... two... one...

When no one approached, I hazarded a surreptitious glimpse over the top of my book, inhaling sharply when I found myself looking into Bailey Cooper's eyes. She immediately looked away and I know I couldn't see it from where she sat across the restaurant with her friends, but the pretty pink blush I knew had spread across her cheeks—tugged at something in me nonetheless.

With a sigh, I turned my attention back to the words in front of me, which were now far less interesting. Concentrating would be harder, anyway, since my ears had decided to take in every clank of silverware and snatch of conversation from surrounding tables, I guess, in hopes of hearing her laughter.

You are not that guy, Showalter.

Now... where was I? Chapter 17.

A shadow fell across my pages.

I ignored it.

The shadow belonged to Stanley, who helped himself to the empty seat across from me. Once he'd settled in, he said in a low voice, "I'm doing this against my will."

I smiled, wryly. "So am I."

"Every Friday, this handsome young gentleman sups alone at the town watering hole," Stanley said, as if he was narrating my biopic. "Though, anyone can see, he could have company if he wanted to."

"He could," I agreed, bidding *An Elegy for the Almost* a silent good night and setting it down.

"Some might take that as a sign that he doesn't want company," Stanley said.

"Some might."

Clasping his hands in front of him, Stanley studied me for a moment and then said, "Why don't you want company, son?"

How to play this? I could put on my toughest voice and say *I'm a lone wolf, Stanley. An alpha without a pack, born to prowl through this life on his own, and I like it that way.* But do I want Stanley's cause of death to be bleeding out on the floor of the Gather & Grill because he fell out of the booth laughing at me and cracked his head open? No.

Honesty? Could I go with honesty?

I scratched my forehead. "The truth is," I began and I kid you not, Cornelia, Ruby, and Iris all shifted in their booth, leaning in our direction. "I hate doing anything by myself. I'm a people person."

Oh, man. Maybe I made the wrong choice because I sounded like I was on a speed date.

Stanley gestured at me to keep going. Cornelia, Ruby, and Iris were miming "go on" at him like he was a child star and they were his momagers.

"But the only thing people in Serenade Creek seem to want to talk about is finding love. And I am... not looking for that."

"Well, just because you're not looking for something doesn't mean it won't find you." He raised his brows at me.

Let me rephrase.

"I am unequivocally not interested in any kind of romantic entanglement. Not now. Not ever."

His brows went higher. "You're what, early 30s?"

"Thirty-three."

He nodded. "Way too young to decide you don't want something now or *ever*."

As I was legitimately on the cusp of proposing we arm wrestle and if I win, he goes back to his own booth, he said, "Listen, son, I don't wanna meddle."

Now I raised my brows. "You don't?"

"I thought I was signing on for a pickleball club, not becoming Stanley of Stanley and the Lovettes."

I don't tell him that if they were the sort of '50s singing quartet with that name, those ladies would not let him be the front man. He'd be the fourth Lovette.

"Son, your bachelorhood is a town crisis at this point," he said. "There's some poor young lady wandering around lonely, and wondering why." He paused and I fought not to let my gaze stray to Bailey. "You're the why, Knox. You've been here a year and haven't yet given in to the magic of Serenade Creek."

I fought the urge to roll my eyes. He sounded just like Jessa, my best friend Luke's fiancée. I actually found my job here because of her. After Luke proposed, Jessa became obsessed with Serenade Creek as the perfect wedding destination. I heard about the love magic from her for two years straight. Then one day I looked up the town out of pure curiosity and found a listing for the assistant principal role at the elementary school. Their guy had just retired. So I applied. On a whim.

And got the call for the interview the next day.

Kismet! Fate! Serendipity! Jessa had cried.

It wasn't any of those things. Because *Kismet! Fate!* and *Serendipity!* aren't real, and neither is magic. It's all just... superstition.

I felt a tug of homesickness. But moving had been the

right thing to do. I'd needed to get out of New York, but I did miss Luke, Jessa, and all our friends.

I'd see them in a few days though. They—and everyone we knew, basically—would be invading Serenade Creek for the wedding of the century. Well, anywhere else, it might be the wedding of the century. Here, I suppose it'll just be one over the top wedding amongst many.

My eyes flicked to Bailey's table. Stanley pounced, twisting to follow my gaze.

"Aha," Stanley said, facing me again with a sly, slow grin.

"No aha." Folding my arms on the table, I shook my head, already scanning for the waitress like she might deliver me from this conversation with a tray of mercy fries.

He leaned in. I winced as he jerked his thumb over his shoulder at Bailey's table. "You see something you like over that way?"

"Stanley." I groaned. "They're not a case of assorted doughnuts at the bakery."

"Some might say they're way sweeter, though," he lifted a shoulder. "All unattached at the moment. You hung out with Bailey Cooper a bit last summer, didn't you?"

I startled, though deep down, I'd been waiting on someone to bring that up. The fact that absolutely no one in this town, where everyone seemed to know everything, seemed to know anything about last summer had puzzled me every day since.

I shoved away the image of her hair highlighted by the moon, the memory of her hand on my shoulder.

"You want me to put in a word with Corn—"

"No," I interrupted, my tone far more abrupt than I'd intended it to be.

My phone lit up as if divine intervention was saving me

—and Stanley—from the foul, foul mood I was falling head-first into.

I glanced at the screen.

My best friend Luke.

Something was wrong, or he'd be texting.

"Sorry, Stanley. I really have to take this."

Stanley was still pressing his case as I slid out of the booth, "But if the one for you is over there, we could have you well on your way to wedded bliss before the Summer Lovin' Festival comes to a close this year. I'm under duress, son. Please just think about it."

"Not happening, Stanley," I said, trying to sound firm and gentle at the same time, but failing on both accounts somehow.

Besides, I wasn't going to be around for that match-making circus this year. Which was a coincidence, but a good one. Smart. Even necessary, maybe. One week last summer was enough to convince me I wasn't dead inside. Two might've made me believe in something dangerous. Like hope.

"Give me one sec, man," I said, accepting Luke's call as I beelined towards the exit, keeping my gaze on that door and nothing else.

Once I was out in the humid, gardenia-soaked night air, I sucked in a couple of breaths and asked, "What's up? Everything o—"

"Jessa is freaking out," he said, his voice so tense I could feel the stress emanating off him even though he was hundreds of miles away. His fiancée wasn't the only one freaking out.

"Tell me what's going on."

Instead of pacing in front of the plate glass windows of

the Gather & Grill, I strode over to a bench tucked up against the exterior of the building and sat, out of the way—and earshot—of any foot traffic.

"She's going to cancel the wedding!"

I swallowed hard. Now wasn't the time for me to revisit old wounds that were now scars. But the words *cancel the wedding* would never not make me nauseous.

Luke wasn't one for histrionics.

I could picture him: Hair sticking up in all different directions from him constantly raking his hands through it. Tie undone and shirt untucked, wrinkled at the hem where he'd been bunching it with his fist. Eyes closed. Jaw working.

"Tell me what happened," I said again. "We'll figure it out."

"She and Rainy got into a massive fight. We're talking... that friendship is done and dusted."

"But those two are like sisters. They've known each other since, what? Junior high."

"Kindergarten," he corrected.

"And there's no chance they're going to make up?"

"Zilch," he said.

Silence stretched between us for a moment.

"Jessa promoted Melody to Maid of Honor but we're still short a bridesmaid. She's convinced it's a bad omen that no one else is willing to stand up for her at the last minute," he said. "I really think she believes it means the whole wedding is cursed."

Oh, boy. Jessa wasn't one for histrionics either.

"Alright. So she's not thinking clearly. She's upset and she has a reason to be. But we're not going to throw out the baby with the bath—"

"Wait, what?" Luke interrupted. "Did you just say something about the baby? How did you know Jessa's pregnant?"

My eyes bulged. Literally. I could feel it. In a way that might induce a migraine.

"She's pregnant?" I whispered. My voice cracked on the word, so permanent, so adult, so... forever.

So something I'd never had. And didn't want.

I reached up with my free hand to massage my temples.

"Shoot." Luke sighed. "I was not supposed to tell anyone that. She's not showing yet. She's been planning this wedding for three years, dude, and she keeps muttering 'odd numbers mean odd outcomes', that everything was planned for pairs, and... I'm..."

He didn't have to say it. He was scared.

Of course he was scared. He was going to be a father.

"So the main issue right now is that the wedding party is uneven?" I asked. I knew I was oversimplifying it by miles. Losing someone you thought was in it for the long haul with you bites. "There is no issue then. You do not even have to ask, man. I'll sit out. Boom, problem solved. Even numbers... even outcomes."

"No. Absolutely not. If I even suggest to her that someone else drop out... No. Not an option. But she got down to asking fourth cousins twice removed or something and then she just kind of... gave up. Said she wasn't going to beg some virtual stranger to participate in what should be the happiest day of her life."

Silence again.

Then finally, he said, "I want this to be the day she's always dreamed of. I want to marry her. I can't imagine not..."

Ugh. That was like a punch to the gut. I knew how he

felt. And how deep it cut to have it so close and watch it slip away.

"Do you want me to talk to Jessa?" I asked, which was grasping at straws, but I had nothing else to offer. And I was good at talking people through meltdowns and break-downs. That was on my resume under Special Skills & Talents.

"No. But there is something you can do."

How Luke had been at my side when I was at my lowest, how he'd single-handedly dragged me back from the brink, wasn't something I needed to remember. It was something I'd never forget.

"Anything, man."

He sniffled. I didn't have to see him to know he was crying. My own eyes welled up. I swiped at them.

"Nothing would restore Jessa's faith like you finding love," he said.

My mouth dropped open. *Stanley, is this you?*

"Excuse me?"

"If you found love again—in *Serenade Creek*, of all places —Jessa would believe it's a sign from the universe. A sign that our wedding was not cursed, but maybe even... blessed."

He waited.

I waited.

I broke first.

"Okay. Just one problem. I haven't found love again." If love repellant was a thing, I'd use it as body spray. Liberally.

"But what if you had?"

"But I haven't."

I waited again. He waited again. This time, he broke first.

"I know this sounds a little wacky, but I hired a professional bridesmaid, who is also willing to pretend to be your girlfriend for the week."

I tugged at my earlobe. Certainly I had not heard him correctly.

"What?"

He repeated what he'd said, slower this time, enunciating every syllable. By the time he was done, I had lost all feeling in my extremities. Vomiting was imminent.

"Okay, well. You're going to have to unhire her, because—"

"You said you'd do anything," he reminded me.

"Oh, Luke. This is an extraordinarily bad idea."

"It's all I've got. This is my only hope," he said, quietly. "You're my only hope."

I closed my eyes.

"You really think she's going to cancel the wedding?"

"I do. She's saying cancel, not postpone, man. You know how Jess is once she makes up her mind. What if she's not just thinking that the wedding is cursed, but the whole marriage is now? We're going to have a kid."

Once again, I was grasping at straws. "Jessa might not want my non-existent girlfriend, whom she's never even heard of, to be one of her bridesmaids—"

"But if she does?"

I threw my head back, looking up at the stars, looking for an answer.

And, I kid you not: One winked.

"And what—" I scrubbed my hand over my face. "In a couple months we just tell Jessa my new boo and I broke up?"

"Amicably," he confirmed.

This was going to go awry. So very awry.

I stood and gave in to the urge to pace.

"There is an upside to this, for you," he said.

"I can't imagine what that might be."

"If you have a girlfriend, you won't have people nagging you all week about why you're still single," he pointed out, just as I turned towards the plate glass window and caught every member of the Hearts & Charts Brigade staring me down from inside the Gather & Grill.

Once again, my attention was drawn, like a magnet, to Bailey.

There was a tightness around her eyes I recognized all too well. A smile that didn't take root in happiness.

My brow creased.

Just as I was, she was in the middle of saying yes to something she wanted to say no to.

She was defaulting to the same autopilot I'd seen her use with pushy PTA moms and overly ambitious fundraiser coordinators. Say yes. Smile. Pretend it's fine. Handle it alone.

I couldn't help her.

But I could help Luke.

So I said yes. Smiled. Pretended it was fine, so he wouldn't have to handle it alone.

CHAPTER THREE

BAILEY

"Baileeeeeeeeeeey," Lyric crooned. I loved that girl, but tonight I was not amused by her tendency to burst into song like life was a musical and she was the star. "Why are you eating that breadstick like you're mad at it?"

Yeah, I had been ripping off bites with my teeth and then chewing with aggression no breadstick deserved. I pointed what was left of it at her. Then at Kelsie. Then at Addison.

Cherish hadn't arrived yet. She was late. She was always late. But tonight, the others were late too—tumbling in ten minutes after we were supposed to meet. Fifteen minutes after I'd arrived.

"Twelve people stopped by this table before y'all got here," I said, narrowing my eyes at her. "Twelve. To either rope me into some town function or offer me condolences like somebody died."

"Somebody died?" Kelsie asked. "Who died? I haven't heard about anybody dying."

Kelsie works at the Serenade Creek Chronicle and though she doesn't cover anything outside of the expansive Wedding section, a reporter at heart, she's always on the lookout for the scoop.

"Nobody died. They were offering their condolences about the Eternal Bouquet."

Addison rolled her eyes and Lyric took it a step further with an eye roll-snort-combo.

"Oh, *that*." Addison reached for the breadbasket with one hand and waved the other dismissively. Easy to be dismissive of the Eternal Bouquet when it wasn't gunning for *your* perpetually single arms.

I leaned forward so no one at another table could over-hear me, though, I wouldn't be telling them anything they didn't already know if they did. "It hit me in the face this time, Addy," I hissed. "I had to fish baby's breath out of my eye."

I then pointed at Kelsie. "Don't you dare laugh."

She held up her hands in surrender, but the struggle was real. Kelsie is more prone to random acts of inappro-priate laughter than anyone I've ever met. If someone had died, odds were, she would giggle at least once during the eulogy.

"Hey, Miss Cooper!"

We all turned towards the voice.

A group of high school kids held court at the family-style table dead center in the Gather & Grill.

Jace McCrae was the one waving at me, calling my name. The quarterback. The golden boy. The one kid everyone would pay attention to.

"The bouquet's gonna work for you this time! I'll be eighteen in a couple months," he hollered.

I raised my hands to auto-cover my burning face but before I could, Lyric grabbed one wrist, Addy the other.

"Unh-uh," Lyric said. "You do not hide yourself because somebody else does something embarrassing."

Kelsie half-stood.

"Kels, don't—"

"Jace McCrae, do you want me to call your mother?" she shouted. "You know I have everybody in this town's phone number in my contacts."

"I am going to die," I said, wondering if Lyric and Addy would let me get away with just... sliding out of my chair and cowering under the table 'til closing time when everybody was gone and I could sneak out. Probably not. "I'm going to die alone. That's what Avalynn heard, by the way." I raised my eyebrows pointedly at Addy, as if it was somehow her fault, just because Avalynn's dad is her best guy friend.

She gasped, looking properly horrified with the second-hand embarrassment she should have. "From who? Not Evan."

"Oh, of course not," Kelsie grabbed Addy's chin and shook it back and forth. "Evan would never say anything less than kind. He's perfect. He's swooooooooony. He's deliciou-uuuuuus."

This right here? Exactly why none of them knew I had a massive crush on Knox.

Addy shook Kelsie off. "It was Gramma Peach, wasn't it?"

I nodded.

"Do you think Gramma Peach was trying to get Evan to ask you out?" Addy asked, looking hurt.

"I'm not interested in Evan," I said at the same time Kelsie and Lyric said, "Bay isn't interested in Evan."

"And Evan isn't interested in me," I said.

Addy laughed, but there wasn't much humor in it. "He's not interested in anybody."

We all went for the breadbasket at the same time and laughed, playfully swatting each other's hands away.

"Only two left," Kelsie said, taking one of the remaining breadsticks, breaking it and handing me half. Lyric dangled the last one toward Addy. They tugged it apart like a wishbone, both grinning.

I heaved a sigh. "Even if Mr. Right showed up and proposed, it'd be too late. I've already used up all my yeses on everybody else."

"Okay, what fresh favor did you agree to before we got here and how do we get you out of it?" Kelsie asked. She tore off a piece of bread and popped it into her mouth.

I ticked it off on my fingers. "Mrs. O'Grady needs a hand at the flea market the first weekend of July—"

"Not your problem," Kelsie said. She winked at me. "Jace McCrae can help her out. I'll sort that for you."

"The Arnault twins want me to look over their portfolios for—"

"You told them they have to pay you, right?" she asked.

I bit my lip, and she knew exactly what that meant.

"Okay, they're gonna pay you. Would you rather do a flat fee or hourly?"

I heard her. I really did. And I wanted to answer.

I glanced toward the door—looking for Cherish, obviously—and instead found Knox walking in. And okay, yes, the sight of him stole my voice for a second. I am *that* lame.

"Flat fee or hourly?" Kelsie asked again.

Lyric spoke up before I could decide. "You know you can say no, right, Bay?"

"And you know I can't. I'm going to go get more breadsticks," I reached for the basket but Addy grabbed it first.

"I'll go. The last week of school always wipes you out."

Lyric leaned over and placed her hand over mine. "You do realize when you say yes to everyone else... you're saying no to yourself, right? It's okay to think about what you want... and what you don't want, sweetie. You need me to put it in song form?"

"Nobody needs that," Kelsie cracked.

Lyric was right, though. She was so right.

"I don't even know what I want anymore," I said, glancing around as if an answer might appear in the air. My eyes landed on Knox. He wasn't seated at his usual booth.

The booth he picked tonight... Did he even remember that the first time he sat there, it was with me?

"Where the heck is Cherish?" Addy demanded, returning with a heaping basket of breadsticks.

Lyric shimmied in her chair. "Carbohydrates make my heart happy, make my heart happy, make my heart happy."

Kelsie popped a breadstick in Lyric's open mouth. Lyric made a face at her, removed the breadstick, and stuck out her tongue.

"I had a thought," Addy said. "You absolutely will not die alone, Bailey."

I laughed. "Well, I like that thought."

"Because we're all going to die alone so we can just die alone together," she finished. She tilted her head, her expression very thoughtful, like she was calculating the logistics.

Kelsie shook her head, her curls flying. "Love all y'all, but I am not planning to hold hands and jump off the top of the belltower with you when we hit sixty."

"Not even if we're all still single?" Addy asked.

"Oh, my word. You are all ridiculous. Number one, there is far more to life than getting married and having kids."

Lyric's hand flew to her heart and she feigned an expression of exaggerated shock. "The Hearts & Charts Brigade is amongst us, Kels," she whispered. "Don't let them hear you say that. You won't have to wait 'til you hit sixty. They'll drag you up the belltower and shove you off *tonight*."

"Also, isn't your job security dependent on people getting married?" I asked. "Where is Cherish and where is our food? I skipped lunch and I'm starving."

"Have another breadstick," Kelsie said. "As I said, Number One, there's more to life than getting married and having kids. BUT. Number Two, we live in Serenade Creek. True Love is going to find us."

"Well, it needs to hurry up. We all turn thirty this summer," she reminded us...as if any of us needed to be reminded.

"This summer is going to be laaaaaame," Lyric sang.

"It won't be lame," Kelsie said. But she poked out her bottom lip for a second. "I hate that we're going to miss our trip though."

Every year since we'd graduated high school, the four of us, and Cherish, had gone on an epic road trip together. It was tradition. It was everything we looked forward to all year. But somehow, this year? One of us was a bridesmaid every single weekend. Well, the odds were against us since Cherish was a professional bridesmaid. But, seriously, except for the five of us, it seemed almost everyone we knew who wasn't already married seemed to be getting married this summer.

I glanced at Knox again.

"There she is!" Addy said.

Cherish barreled toward us, waving like we were a bus pulling away without her.

"Oh. My. Goodness." She practically fell into the empty chair next to me. "What a day."

"You're late," Lyric told her.

"Very late," I said.

She fished around in her purse and pulled out a packet of strawberry jelly. Then she unwrapped her silverware, put the napkin in her lap, and brandished the butter knife. "I have a good reason. Give me a sec."

While she jellied her breadstick, Kelsie said, "How do you run a business where punctuality is arguably the most important quality to have?"

Cherish took a massive bite, chewed like she hadn't eaten in days, then casually hijacked my sweet tea. Lyric raised her eyebrows at me.

"I'm never late to a gig," she said. "And I'm not that late tonight. Everybody knows the Gather & Grill is notoriously slow."

"That's by design so that you have time to *gather*," I pointed out.

She waved her hand dismissively and if one more person waves their hand dismissively, I might yank it off their wrist and smack them with it.

Clenching my jaw, I snuck another peek at Knox.

He was reading. I squinted but I couldn't tell what the book was.

At that exact moment, he looked up. Our eyes met. I whipped my head back towards Cherish, who was flashing us her most dazzling smile. Her *I Need A Favor* smile.

"Speaking of gigs," she said, which I guess we kind of had been? She bounced in her seat a bit. "I have the opportunity of a lifetime for one of you ladies."

"Hard pass," I said. "I've had more than enough lifetime opportunities, thanks."

Lyric clapped. "So proud of you, Bay-Bay."

"Don't call me that."

"Standing up for yourself all over the place!" she grinned at me.

Cherish rapped on the table with her free hand. "You guys. Hello! This is serious. I just double booked myself."

"One might argue that that's worse than being late," Addy pointed out.

"Listen. I have a wedding tomorrow, a wedding Sunday evening, a wedding on Wednesday—not going to judge, but why does anyone choose a Wednesday to get married?—a morning wedding and an evening wedding next Saturday, which is gonna be tricky. Then another one next Sunday. BUT. This guy just called me and he is totally desperate, but it's a major conflict."

"Not it!" Kelsie shook her head.

"I do not volunteer as tribute," Addy said.

"No, no, no, no, no, no, no, no, no, no," Lyric sang to the tune of Here Comes the Bride. She nudged me hard in the ribs with her elbow as Cherish's pleading eyes landed on me.

"Oh, heck no," I said. "I'm not going anywhere near another wedding. I mean. Other than the two I have to go to because I'm in them. But until August? You are not catching this girl within two hundred feet of that Infernal Bouquet. I may take out an official restraining order."

"Listen. The groom called me, desperate as I said—"

"Not my problem," I said.

"Good girl," Kelsie mouthed at me. Lyric gave me another round of applause.

Cherish looked slightly taken aback but after a brief pause, forged ahead undeterred.

Over Cherish's shoulder, I spotted Stanley sliding into Knox's new booth, leaving the Brigade behind. Matchmaking business. Official and ominous.

It felt like someone reached into my chest and gave my heart a warning squeeze.

Where was he going this summer? Maybe he had a girlfriend back in New York, where he was from, and was going to spend time with her? At least he wasn't bringing her here, I guess?

"Bailey, please at least listen?" Cherish begged.

"Okay, okay." I pulled my attention back to her, grateful to stop indulging my inner teenage drama queen.

"The bride and her bestie's friendship turned into an endship. From what the groom said, there was major emotional carnage. The week of the wedding. The bride is devastated and threatening to cancel the wedding she's been planning for three years."

Lyric shook her head almost imperceptibly at me as if to say *Do not fall for it.*

"I mean, can you imagine?" Cherish shuddered. "Two of us having that kind of falling out the week of one of our weddings? That we'd been planning for three years?"

She was tugging at my heartstrings—and maybe a few guilt strings for good measure.

I would resist. I had to resist.

"Two of us would never have a falling out like that," Kelsie said. "Because the other three would handcuff the two idiots together 'til they came to their senses."

Addy nodded. "Facts."

"Well, anyway, I guess the bride didn't have as dedicated and slightly unhinged friend group as I do. Anyway, they're going to be in town for the entire week and have a ton of events planned and they're going to need someone who can be boots on the ground from Sunday, when they arrive, to the following Sunday morning when they leave. The actual wedding is Saturday night."

"Wait," Lyric shook her head. "Hold up. And you told the guy you would do it? Even though you... very much can't?"

"I felt so bad for him! I had to!" Cherish finished off my tea.

"But you can't do it!" Lyric—very reasonably—pointed out.

"But one of you can!" Cherish cried. "They couldn't find a replacement and without one, the bride really might call the whole thing off."

"Well, I couldn't if I wanted to because I'm babysitting Avalynn for Evan all week," Addy lifted a shoulder.

Cherish wagged a finger at Addy. "I'm going to confirm that with him, ma'am."

"And I'm kind of in the wedding business, too," Lyric said. She owns a record store and creates bespoke playlists for events, usually the kind of events where people walk down the aisle and say *I do*. "I am booked solid this week. I can't just close up shop, even for a day."

I had a sick feeling in my stomach.

"Kels?" Cherish pouted at her and batted her eyes.

Kelsie shook her head. "I have to fly to Montana on Wednesday, remember?"

"Oh, boo," Cherish said.

Then she looked at me again.

"Say no, say no, say no," Lyric chanted.

"Kindly butt out," Cherish smiled at her beatifically. "Let me paint the whole picture before you make up your mind, Bay."

"You're not going to reel her in with art metaphors," Kelsie said.

"You'll get the full pay. It's a lot," Cherish said. She pulled a pen and piece of paper out of her purse, jotted down a number, and slid it towards me.

I groaned. Were my eyeballs drooling or crying conflicted tears?

On one hand, that was soooooooooo much money. On the other hand, I really, really, really wanted to spend the next week holed up in my apartment where I wouldn't have to see anyone or talk to anyone or put on pants.

"You could raid the Clover art store like it's Black Friday and come out with every fancy paint you've ever drooled over."

I wouldn't have to scrimp and save to make rent, either. Maybe the nightmares about fighting rabid raccoons for the last croissant in the trash can outside the bakery would come to an end.

My tummy felt like a cauldron full of nausea being rapidly stirred.

I shook my head. "Cher, I'm sorry—"

"No, you are not," Lyric said. "You have nothing to be sorry about."

"I just can't," I said. "I need a break from everyone and their commentary about the bouquet."

"I get it," she said. "I do. I'll just tell the guy no. But it sure is a bummer that there's this opportunity for one of us to get to spend a week at the Enchanted Rose Inn and none of us can."

We all gasped.

Our favorite server, Ryder, chose that moment to arrive with our food and he probably thought we'd all gotten so weak from hunger we could no longer move, because, except for Cherish, we were statues.

"Thank you," Cherish told Ryder as he sat her burger down in front of her. Then she dug in, taking a ginormous bite.

It took her a few minutes to realize we were all still staring at her and that even though we all had food now, none of us were eating.

"Dang, we don't have any ketchup. I might have a pack or two in my ..." her voice trailed off. She looked at each of us in turn. "What?"

"Did you..." Addy began.

"Is the..." Lyric shook her head.

"I think..." Kelsie, too, lost her words.

We were all starstruck. Over a building.

"Is the wedding you need help with at the Enchanted Rose Inn?" I demanded.

Cherish nodded slowly. "Yeah, that was one of the very first things I said about the gig."

We all shook our heads.

"No. No, I think we would all remember that," Addy said.

"We definitely would," Kelsie agreed. "Ugh! Do you know they won't even let me in with my press credentials? I have pitched so many interviews with the owners and they say nope every time. Unless you're a guest, you can't come onto the property."

"And it's booked into eternity, basically," Addy added, sadly.

Into eternity and only for weddings.

I sighed. "I can't believe that out of all the eighty-five-hundred weddings we've been in and to collectively, none of them have been *there*."

We were all born in Serenade Creek but none of us had ever stepped foot inside the Enchanted Rose Inn. Just as hardcore Disney fans likely all have spending the night inside Cinderella's Castle on their bucket list, staying at the Enchanted Rose Inn is on all of ours.

"You should have led with that," Lyric said. "I probably would've considered selling my store and starting anew with another career after the wedding's over."

"If I got inside the Enchanted Rose, I would never leave," Addy said. "I wonder if I could put Avalynn in my suitcase and sneak her in?"

I looked at Kelsie who was seriously looking like she might bail on her cousin's wedding in Montana. She looked back at me as if to say, *You've got dibs but if you say no...*

"So... if one of us agreed to do it, we'd not only get a serious payday, we'd get to stay, for an entire week, at the Enchanted Rose?" I asked.

Cherish nodded. "And, I don't want to twist your arm, but the groom said the whole place is booked with just their wedding party and guests. All from out of town. You know the staff aren't tacky enough to say anything about the you-know-what... so you might go the whole blissful week without hearing a word about it."

"Unless the bride is using the Eternal Bouquet, in which case it will probably smack me in the face again," I said, but we all knew I was going to do it. Not just because I'm Bailey

Always Says Yes, but because... it was the Enchanted Rose Inn. I wasn't lying when I said I didn't know what I wanted anymore. But this? This I wanted.

I glanced over at Knox's booth. He was gone. Just like my burgeoning resolve to say no.

CHAPTER FOUR

BAILEY

"This is amazing," Cherish whispered in an excited but reverent hush. "Look at the view of the mountains from here. Soooo pretty! Just being on the grounds raises your serotonin. I can literally feel my pores tightening."

"I feel something tightening," I muttered as she patted her cheeks. "Probably the early stages of a stress-induced back spasm."

My duffel bag was too heavy, like it was packed with bricks and misgivings. I adjusted the strap on my shoulder.

Cherish practically skipped past me, blissfully unconcerned with my plight. "You're not going to regret agreeing to do this!"

The courtyard of the Enchanted Rose Inn was everything I'd dreamed, and more, but unfortunately the breathtaking scenery blurred in my periphery like an abstract painting, distorted by lack of sleep and sheer panic.

I *already* regretted saying yes to this.

This, and all of the life choices I'd made that led me here, with all of my internal organs undulating with dread.

Up ahead, Cherish spun in a slow circle before pretty much floating toward the grand entrance. The afternoon sun spilled across the path like liquid gold. The landscaping was straight out of a classy wedding planner's fever dream—twinkle lights in the hedges, at least three gazebos, and roses climbing anything that stood still for longer than three seconds, their scent so rich and heady it felt like you could get drunk on it... Oh, my goodness, I hope those roses don't bouquet themselves and start hurtling towards my head.

And... how sad is it that I just might be developing flowerphobia?

Cherish stopped in front of the fountain.

"The real live Fountain of Forever, Bay!" she announced. "I can't—"

Her phone went off, blaring Going To The Chapel so loud I was half surprised the peace police didn't pop out behind a shrub and write her a ticket for noise pollution.

She yanked it from her pocket, silenced it with a grimace, and made a face like she'd bitten into a lemon.

Instead of catching up to her, I stopped, too. I had to put this duffel of doom down for a second. I couldn't help but stare.

The courtyard dropped a few shallow steps, and there it was, in the center of the recessed stage. A wide stone basin ringed in carved scrollwork, with three stacked scalloped bowls rising from the middle, water spilling quietly from one to the next.

It looked unassuming enough but its legend was heavy: Toss a coin in and it doesn't grant a wish—it tells the universe you're ready. For love. For forever. For *everything*.

Cherish groaned.

"What's wrong?" I asked, rolling my shoulders. "Did they cancel the wedding? Can we just take a quick look-see around inside and head home?"

She gave me a sharp look. "Bailey Cooper, you could jinx a wedding by even thinking such a thing! Take it back." Then she sighed. "Speaking of jinxed weddings, though, the king of them, A.K.A. my dad, is in town. Wants to get lunch."

"That's good... right?" I asked, cautiously. Cherish's relationship with her dad was... tumultuous.

"It sounds good until I'm sitting in the booth alone, stalking his socials, and realizing he forgot we had plans again because he's rented a bicycle built for two and taken Wife Number Four on a ride around the park. Which I'll find out about when I see they've posted a selfie with the caption *'so lucky to be loved by this one, hashtag in tandem for life.'* Blah blah blah vomit."

"I'm sorry, Cherish."

"Do I say yes, or tell him I died?" She slipped her phone back into her pocket. "There's only one way to decide this. Shoot. I left my purse in the car. Hook me up, please."

"Sooner or later, you're going to have to stop outsourcing your emotional decisions to spare change," I said, but I was already digging in my own purse for a quarter for Cherish to flip. I always kept a bunch of them in case a kid was short for the vending machine, or, you know, my bestie had to decide whether to tell her dad she was dead or not.

"Heads I go, tails I say no," she said, cupping her hands in front of her to catch the coin I was about to toss.

A blur of red zipped past my face and I shrieked, hopping back like it was a live grenade.

The quarter slipped from my fingers, arced beautifully over Cherish's shoulder, and then—

Nothing.

No clink.

No ping.

No satisfying tink-tink-tink as the coin skittered across the stone path.

Just... silence.

"Where did it go?" I whispered. "Did you hear it land?"

Cherish shook her head. "No, but objects don't just vanish mid-air. It could've hit the grass... way over there or... maybe it went into a shrub... or..."

Her voice trailed off as we both turned slowly toward the fountain.

"No. Absolutely not. Nope. I rebuke this in the name of my sanity. No, no, no, no."

"Except maybe yes?" she said, wide-eyed. "I think you just yeeted your penny into the Fountain of Forever."

"It was a quarter, not a penny, but besides the point: I didn't yeet anything!"

"Hey," she came over and grabbed my arm. "This might be a good thing! Maybe this is why the Eternal Bouquet hasn't worked for you before! Because the universe didn't think you were ready, but now that you've told it differently—"

"I. Did. Not. Tell. The. Universe. Anything."

Suddenly light-headed, I swatted her hand away. The gossip after the Eternal Bouquet had been wrong about me five times was bad enough, but... if word got out that the Fountain of Forever refused my declaration of readiness...

Ugh... if anyone even heard that I tossed a coin in the Fountain, I'd sound so desperate.

"You know what?" I cried. "I'm over Serenade Creek and all of its silly superstitions. That's all they are. They aren't magic and you know what else? I'm pretty sure cardinals are stalking me and—"

"Bailey." Cherish was waving at me. "BAILEY. BAILEY!"

I glanced in the direction she was jerking her head.

One of the Enchanted Rose's many side doors had swung open.

A guy I didn't recognize stepped out and rushed towards us.

But he could've had two heads and I wouldn't have noticed.

I was looking at the person behind him.

Knox.

He stepped into the sunlight, looking every bit like a man hand-delivered by fate, with cinematic timing so perfect I was half-expecting a dramatic soundtrack to kick in.

I froze.

He froze.

Our eyes locked like magnets, and for one long, impossible second, it felt like the entire world held its breath.

"Bailey?"

I didn't hear him say my name as much as I saw the question in his expression as his mouth formed the word.

"Hello! I'm Luke Griffith. Which one of you is Cherish Bloom?" the other guy—who may or may not have two heads —asked.

"What are you doing here?" Knox and I asked each other at the same time. Like we'd practiced.

"Oh! That's me," Cherish called. "I'm Cherish, but let me explain. There's been a slight change of plans and my

amazing associate here is going to be your bridesmaid! Bailey
is—"

"A teacher at my school," Knox cut in sharply. "We can't
fake date."

I took a horrified step back and bumped into a wrought-
iron shepherd's hook, sending a lantern swinging.

"I'm sorry, we can't *what now?*"

Cherish gasped, hands flying to her mouth. "Oh no. Oh
no, no, no—"

I turned on her, eyes wide and voice rising through
clenched teeth. "I do not like those oh nos, Cherish Bloom."

"Uh, okay." She folded her perfectly manicured hands
in front of her with the calm poise of a flight attendant
about to tell you the plane's on fire. "Luke and, er, um,
Knox, Bailey and I just need two minutes to chat in private
and—"

"We don't have two minutes," Luke said, raking his hand
through his hair. He glanced over his shoulder at the front
door and whispered, "Jessa was right behind us and she
cannot... hear any of this."

I glanced at Knox.

"Jessa is the bride," he said.

"The bride who is gonna murder me if she finds out I
paid someone to be her bridesmaid," Luke hissed. "You
promised me discretion."

"Wait. The bride doesn't even know you hired a professional bridesmaid?" I took a step forward, my voice sharp.
My pulse felt like it was about to take flight and never come
back. I needed to sit down but my options were a very expen-
sive looking planter or the ground.

Knox's eyes were downcast, his hands shoved in his
pockets. Luke was glancing back and forth between us and

the front of the Enchanted Rose with such frequency, he was going to strain a neck muscle.

"Is she serious? Are you serious? No, the bride does not know. The bride thinks the best man's girlfriend stepped up to be her bridesmaid," Luke said and now he had a whole vein in the forehead thing going on. His eyes bulged at Cherish. "How long have you been doing this? Would I have been better off if I'd just rented a ferret off Craigslist to do this for me?"

"Hey. Don't be a jerk," Knox said.

Luke blew out a breath. "I'm sorry, I just... I am not in a good place right now."

And that makes... the whole lot of us.

"Oh, no. Oh, shoot. Okay. Just give me a sec," Cherish said.

"We don't have—"

"Why don't you go waylay Jess?" Knox suggested, as calm and capable as always.

"Please straighten this out. If she doesn't murder me, I might have a coronary at this point. Oh—and at this point, I don't care which one of you stays, but we already told Jessa Knox's girlfriend's name is Cherish, so... whoever stays is Cherish for the week!" With a shake of his head, Luke turned and power walked back to the entrance.

Cherish immediately launched into orbit. "I... may have forgotten to tell you part of your duties, Bay! There was a lot happening! But, uh, yeah, Luke has upgraded to our all-inclusive package where, you, ah, not only fill in as a brides-maid, but you act as the best man's girlfriend to, ah, make the experience seamless. Immersive. To better integrate yourself with the, uh, wedding party. And... I guess the best man is... Assistant Principal Knox? I didn't know that. But yay, you know each other! That'll make it less awkward. Right? Right?"

Words. She was saying words. And I knew most of them.

But I was barely paying attention to her.

I'd had front row tickets to so many of Cherish's hare-brained and not-so-logically thought-out schemes over the years, I knew what she'd done probably made total sense to her in the moment and once the decision was made, she hadn't really thoughtfully examined all of the many, many potential fallouts. Or, thought about them at all.

"Knox!" I cried. "You were in on this?"

He winced, and ran a hand over his jaw. "I was roped into it."

"You are the same guy who lectured me about my ability to say no two days ago, right? So you do know that's a thing you can do?"

"I wouldn't say I lectured you, but... That's beside the point. Listen. I was against this too. I *am* against this. But.... sometimes the ends justify the means."

I raised my eyebrows. "Do they?"

"I would do anything for Luke."

I got that, that level of ride-or-die with a friend, but... this was so wrong and I was... disappointed in Knox.

He was supposed to be the solid one. Mr. Maturity. The guy who didn't let people twist him into a balloon animal version of himself.

No. I had no right. None. Zero. No right at all to have an opinion about what this man did in his personal life, insofar as it had no bearing on his ability to be the world's best assistant principal.

I squared my shoulders. "Well, fortunately for us, I don't have that undying loyalty to Luke, so—"

"Bailey!" Cherish squeaked.

Shaking my head slowly, I said, "You're just going to have to give Luke a full refund or whatever, Cherish. And then we're leaving."

I felt her stare, pleading and silent.

I glanced at Knox.

"I meant what I said, Bailey. You give a lot. You do not have to do this, if you don't want to," he said, quietly.

Ugh, what's that feeling in my chest? My heart growing a size or two?

I wanted to say no.

I swallowed hard.

I think I wanted to say no.

But somewhere, in the back of my head, in the place where I keep all my bad ideas stored under lock and key, a little voice whispered: *Serenade Creek's love-magic is giving you another week with the man of your dreams, you moron!*

All right, maybe it was more of a wail than a whisper.

He's not the man of my dreams! And I'm disappointed in him right now! Even if I have no right to be!

Was I arguing with myself? Yes. Yes, I was.

And even if I said no, even if we moved Knox from the equation altogether, I would spend the whole next week drowning in the guilt of letting Cherish down.

"Bailey?" Knox prompted. Gently. Softly. Like the ooey, gooey cinnamon roll of a man he was.

I rubbed at my temple, suddenly very aware that I was stress-sweating. Fabulous.

"Shh, she's processing," Cherish said.

Lyric's words popped back into my head: *It's okay to think about what you want... and what you don't want, sweetie.*

My heart pounded. Every beat felt like a 'no' I wanted to say, but it was trapped in my chest.

However...

What if they weren't nos? What if they were just yesses that were scared?

Then:

"OH, MY GOODNESS!"

A woman with what could only be described as Big Bride Energy came careening down the steps leading from the Enchanted Rose's grand entrance as if she'd been shot out of a cannon. She wore a head-to-toe glow, a tennis skirt and neon-white sneakers like she'd just jogged here from the set of a bridal fitness video.

She skidded to a halt when she got within a few feet of us.

Her blonde curls still bouncing, she looked from me to Cherish and back again. Then she grinned a slightly manic, slightly wobbly grin. "So... which one of you is our Knoxxy's new boo and... who is the extra because..."

Her voice trailed off and thank heavens Luke was standing behind her, because I kid you not, her knees looked five seconds away from buckling and her eyes kind of rolled back in her head for a moment.

Next to me, Cherish gasped. "Are you alright?"

Jessa held out her hands as if to say *I'm fine, it's fine, everything's fine*. "Just a little peckish... and I really can't handle any extra guests, no offense. So..."

I stared at the rose-gray stonework beneath my feet. It shimmered in the sun like it had been dusted with gold glitter. But... why did it feel spongy?

"I promise you will thank me for this later," Cherish whispered. "This is Cherish," she said to Jessa. "I'm just her

BFF and ride. And I'm going to get out of your gorgeous hair now. Have an amazing wedding!"

Then she pulled me into a hug, like she wasn't going to see me again for ten years and whispered, "The love train is leaving the station and you've got the ticket. Enjoy the ride!"

Wait, what?

She nodded her head not-so-subtly at Knox and gave me a wink.

"There's no such thing as a coincidence in Serenade Creek, Bailey."

She let me go.

"Bye, now!" she waggled her fingers at everyone, whipped around, and all but ran back to the path leading off the grounds.

A breeze blew through, tousling my hair, and it was hard to believe, but even the air here smelled *romantic*.

"Cherish!" Jessa squealed.

I glanced back towards Cherish, who didn't stop—then I realized, of course, Jessa wasn't talking to that Cherish. She was talking to me.

She enveloped me in an embrace that felt more like a headlock, if I'm being honest. "Honey. You are saving my wedding. My marriage. My life. I cannot put into words how grateful I am for you stepping up like this. And Knox!" she pulled back and held me at arm's length. "I don't know how you found the key to unlock his heart, but..."

She placed her hand over her heart, tears glistening in the corners of her eyes as she looked at me like I was a miracle. "You did the impossible, girlie. I didn't think he'd ever find love again. You must be something really special."

I glanced at Knox. Was he blushing? He held my gaze but looked mighty uncomfortable.

Jessa beamed. "Let's get you inside and introduce you to everyone, huh?"

So I did what I always do. I smiled. I nodded. I let myself be ushered inside.

But my brain was buffering, my shirt was sticking to me in weird places, and oh, right—I was now pretending to be my best friend, fake-dating my boss, and about to spend the next week trapped in a real-life rom-com with a man I couldn't have. A man I shouldn't want...but did.

CHAPTER FIVE

Bailey.

In a town that believes love is magic, Bailey Cooper had been cast in the role of my pretend girlfriend.

It was almost enough to make me believe in fate.

Almost.

Man, she was beautiful. Everything about her...

She stood frozen in the lobby of the inn, her gaze flitting upward, as if she was admiring the chandeliers but it was more likely she was seeking an escape hatch with a rope ladder dangling down for her to grab onto.

Her features were twisted into a stricken expression.

She was tormented and I felt it as much as I saw it.

Luke rocked back and forth on his heels, his hands clasped behind his back, his eyes like ping-pong balls. Jessa was chirping away, oblivious.

"Hey!" I said, my too loud voice only amplified by the ridiculously high ceilings.

Everyone startled, jerking their attention to me.

"I haven't even gotten to say a proper hello to my girl this morning," I said. Then for Luke and Jessa's benefit, I added, "Excuse me."

I strode towards Bailey with my arms out. She took a step back.

My back to the happy couple, I mouthed *"It's okay"* at her.

The first time I'd hugged her, she'd melted into my arms. I'd always thought that expression hyperbolic and cheesy until it was me holding her.

But that was a year ago. A year that might as well have been a lifetime ago.

This time?

She tensed, her whole body going rigid, as I wrapped her in an embrace.

"It's okay," I whispered into her hair, which smelled like sunshine and candy. "I'm going to get us through this, alright?"

It was a big promise, but an unwavering determination rose in me to see it through.

She didn't say anything. Just kind of wiggled until I let her go.

Her discomfort was palpable in the air: I'd made things worse, not better.

I stepped away. Scratched my jaw.

Keep your hands to yourself from now on, man.

If I'd known. If I'd had any inkling that Bailey would be the woman showing up here to be my fake better half... I would have shut it down. I would have told Luke no. Unequivocally. This was a line I wouldn't have crossed, not even for him.

"Hey," I said again, this time in a low, purposeful tone that wouldn't be an attack on everyone's already frazzled nerves. "Jessa, I know you're eager to introduce everyone to Bailey, but—"

"Bailey?" Jessa's eyes narrowed at me—I'd stepped right in it. "Who is Bailey?"

I don't know whose eyes were wider—Bailey's or Luke's. They both seemed to have lost all capacity to blink.

"Oh, ah..."

Say something!

But their collective panic had latched onto me like a barnacle and... what are words?

"I'm Bailey," Bailey said, finally.

Luke clutched his chest.

Was he actually going to have a coronary?

I held my breath. Bailey glanced from Jessa to Luke to me and back to Jessa.

She smiled a tight smile. "Knox just calls me Cherish because... he... cherishes me."

I exhaled, my face breaking into a grin.

Bailey Cooper is brilliant.

"Awww, that's so sweet!" Jessa cried. "Knoxxy! That frozen heart of yours has melted, hasn't it?"

Oh, how I hated when she called me that. Also: How she sometimes spoke about me as if I was the Grinch who stole love.

I avoided Bailey's questioning stare.

"As I was saying, I know you're eager to introduce everyone to Bailey... Cherish... the Bailey I cherish..." What was I saying? I cleared my throat. "But why don't we give her a few minutes to get settled?"

"That would be great, actually," Bailey said.

"I'll take your things up, honey."

"Thanks, *honey*." She said it with an edge, like it was a euphemism for something that tasted bad.

Okay. Duly noted. Don't call her honey.

I hoisted her bag back over my shoulder. "What room is she in, Jess?

Jessa laughed. "Uh, she's in your room, silly."

She stopped laughing. "What's wrong?"

I glanced at Bailey, who looked like Jessa had just informed her she'd be sharing a hot tub with piranhas.

"Um." Bailey.

"I..." Me.

"What. Is. Wrong?" Jessa demanded. "Luke told me you two live together, so I figured you'd want to stay together here, too? Besides—"

"We do not live together!" Bailey blurted.

"Sweetums, I told you they live in the same apartment building, not the same apartment," Luke said, quickly.

I was 100% certain that is not what he'd told her. He was taking his life in his own hands by giving false testimony. But the glare she was giving him would've made lesser men confess to capital crimes.

"But you know how many things are on your mind!" he went on, while Bailey and I watched. I wondered if she, too, was wondering how deep he was going to dig this hole, which Jessa was likely to bury us all in. "You must've misunderstood."

Bailey inhaled sharply.

If Jessa's eagle eyes wouldn't have certainly caught it, I would've mouthed *I'm sorry* at her. I was so sorry.

"Well," Jessa's voice was clipped. "There are no more rooms at the inn, so—"

"No worries!" Bailey said. "None at all. I live ten minutes away. I don't have to stay here to be in the wedding. I can just go home each night and—"

"Absolutely not!" Jessa yelped as if Bailey had bitten her. She closed her eyes. "Deep breaths. Deep breaths." When she opened her eyes again, she smiled beatifically. Her voice was serene. She took a few steps over to Bailey. "Bailey. Woman to woman. The guys don't get it, but you do, right? How important it is, how vital, for every detail of a girl's wedding to be... everything she'd dreamed of. I designed our wedding to take place in a bubble. If someone is coming and going, that's going to burst the bubble. I implore you, Bailey. Don't burst my bubble."

Bailey made a choking sound. "I don't—"

Luke's gaze—*do something, do something!*—bore into the side of my face. I couldn't tear my eyes away from Bailey, as I helplessly watched her soul leave her body. I indeed needed to do something but her overwhelm was overwhelming me.

"Okay, I need someone to explain to me what the big deal is, please. Do you and Knox not ever spend the night at each other's places, Bailey?"

"Jessa," Luke said, gently. "Sweetums, don't make it weird. We don't need to know their sleeping arrangements."

"We do this week! Oh, my gosh. I am so sorry. I'm just... very, very stressed. And peckish. And you told me they were in a long-term, committed relationship, so I'm just trying to figure out why the energy in the room is like I'm trying to march them handcuffed together to the guillotine! Does Knoxxy snore?" Jessa asked. "Is that it? Because I want all of my bridesmaids bright-eyed and bushy-tailed, so if that's it, tell me and we can get him some of those strips to put on his nose or some noise-canceling headphones with a soothing playlist for you?"

"Jessa!" Thankfully, I finally found my voice. "Could you take about three steps back and give her some space? You're kind of in her face."

"Sorry! I'm so sorry. I'm a monster. I'm a bridezilla. I'm a total—"

"It's fine," Bailey said. "It's... everything will be fine."

The panic that had been flickering across her face hardened into a smooth and polite acceptance. The quiet kind you wear when you know the train's already left the station and the only thing to do now is hang on and hope for snacks.

My chest tightened in a way I couldn't ignore. Maybe I was the one on a collision course with a coronary.

"What room are we in?" Bailey asked. Her voice was warm, but her eyes were cold.

I pointed towards the side stairs. "Room Seventeen."

"See you guys in a bit?" Jessa called after us.

I held up my hand in a wave of acknowledgment before following Bailey silently upstairs.

"Third floor," I told her, but once we hit the landing between the second and third, I said, "Hey, stop a second."

She turned around and faced me. Her eyes were glassy with unshed tears. "What?"

This was not okay. Not even within the realm of okay.

"Listen. Wait here. I'm going to go keep a look out and the second the lobby is clear, we're getting you out of here."

"What?" she asked again.

"You don't have to be here. You don't have to explain anything to anyone. You're an innocent bystander here. Let's get you home and I'll deal with the fallout."

She didn't laugh as much as she barked out a single, humorless, "Ha."

Folding her arms across her stomach, she frowned. Then she said, "Did you see Jessa? She's about five minutes from full-on emotional collapse. I've been there. I'm not going to ruin her wedding. We're in this." She heaved a sigh. "For better or for worse."

With a shake of her head and slightly slumped shoulders, she started back up, one slow step at a time, with me on her heels.

By the time we were in the room, though, the pendulum had swung in the other direction.

"I cannot do this," she said. "I cannot do this."

She paced the length of the rug, muttering it under her breath over and over.

"You don't have to," I said.

Turning to me, she asked, "If I bolt, do you really think Jessa will cancel the wedding?"

The look in her eyes...

I raked a hand through my hair. Scratched the back of my head. Shoved both hands in my pockets. Anything to quell the itchiness in my fingers.

You have no right to touch her, not even in comfort. Don't even consider it again.

"It's not your problem, Bailey. It really isn't—"

"It is now," she said quietly. "If I leave, my stomach will be in knots for the next seven days because Cherish will be mad at me and... I won't know if everything was okay with Luke and Jessa and I won't be able to eat or sleep. I'll just..."

She didn't finish.

I waited.

There was more coming. I had to give her time.

She walked slowly around the suite, not pacing this time, but taking it all in. "It's something else," she murmured.

Then she spun around. Took a deep breath. "I can't do this. Not with you."

I opened my mouth but she held up a hand.

"When I agreed to this... I didn't know the bride wasn't looped in. And I certainly would not have said yes if I had known I was going to have to fake date someone. Especially if I knew that someone was *you*."

It was Bailey. She hadn't intended to fire the kill shot, but boy, if her aim wasn't true.

I winced and she saw it and I hated that she saw it. The last thing I wanted was to give her something else to feel misplaced guilt over.

She took a deep breath. She was steeling herself for something.

I waited. I'd wait as long as I had to. Patience wasn't something I'd ever taken issue with.

I watched as she pressed her lips together. Fiddled with her hair.

Outside, a bird was singing: *Purdy purdy purdy.*

Bailey narrowed her eyes and muttered something. She walked over to the window seat. Sat down. "Okay. I won't have to see you again 'til the end of August, so... hopefully either I'll die of embarrassment by then or you'll get amnesia." Another deep breath. "Last summer meant something to me, Knox. I don't want another pretend week with you."

Oh. *Oh.*

She met my eyes with such an intensity it was like she was daring herself not to look away and the stakes were high. I couldn't look away either, but...

I said nothing.

But there was so much I wanted to say.

That I remembered every second of that week. Couldn't forget a detail if I tried.

That it hadn't just meant something to me. It had meant everything.

Last summer still lived like marrow in my bones and this woman in front of me? She'd cracked things open in me I'd sworn I'd never feel again. Things I didn't think I *could* feel again.

Bailey nodded, even though I hadn't said anything for her to agree with.

"So here's what we'll do because I cannot be with you 24/7," she said. "I know it's not what Jessa wants, but each night, you'll help me sneak out after everyone has gone to sleep and then each morning you'll sneak me back in at the crack of dawn. Easy peasy. No one will notice."

She looked so determined. So hopeful.

I swallowed hard.

"That might be sustainable... if we were staying at an establishment that cared a little bit less about who comes and goes."

Her face fell. "Like maybe the White House. Well, that was a stupid plan. Cherish and I practically had to each sign over a kidney to get on grounds."

"It wasn't stupid," I said. She leveled me with a don't-you-dare-patronize-me glare. In that moment, I would've sworn on my life that I would not do anything this week to hurt this creative, funny, beautiful, big-hearted woman or lead her on. "It wasn't well thought out, maybe. But hey. Between us, we've got four kidneys, yeah? If sneaking you in every night and out every morning is what makes you comfortable, that's what we'll do."

Whatever happened last summer between us, it had been temporary. It had started out temporary. Then I'd reiterated, after the fact, that it couldn't ever be anything more.

I'd firmly shut that door. But every time I saw her again, it threatened to creak back open a little. I couldn't ever tell her that. And I couldn't let myself give in to it. It would only hurt her more.

I owed her not to give her any kind of mixed signals.

And just like on that first day we met, she laid out ground rules.

"Okay," she said, standing. "Well. We're going to need boundaries. No unnecessary touching, for starters."

"Got it." If I had to walk around for the next seven days with my hands so deep in my pockets I could pull up my socks, I'd do it.

"Absolutely no terms of endearment. No sweetheart, no baby, no honey."

While she paced, I perched on the edge of the bed.

"And absolutely no kissing."

I'd already assumed kissing went under no unnecessary touching, but I didn't question her.

"No long, lingering looks."

I waited.

"I would say no sleeping in the same bed, but I'm not sleeping here, so that won't be an issue. I still think this is very, very wrong. It's not like we're teenagers who have paid the popular girl to go to prom with our nerdy cousin. Not that that wouldn't be wrong, because that would be wrong on so many levels. But we're adults. This is... real life. The most important day of real life."

She looked at me. Really looked at me.

"How did you get roped into this?"

I sighed. "It's a long story."

"That's what people say about stories they don't want to tell." She paused. She was right. "How long have you known Luke?"

"Since middle school. Jessa since our freshman year of college. She was my roommate's sister. I introduced her and Luke."

"Well, if they were meant to be, someone had to." Bailey shrugged. "Why didn't he just tell her he was hiring a professional bridesmaid?"

"She wouldn't have gone for it. I know that makes it sound worse…"

"That doesn't make it *sound* worse, Knox. That actually *does* make it worse."

She plucked the wedding itinerary off the table inside the doorway. Flipped through the pages. Her eyes went wide.

Glancing over at me, she asked, "Have you looked through this?"

"Scanned it."

"Do you know what we're doing this afternoon?"

"From the look on your face, I'm guessing couples massages?"

Bailey wagged a finger at me. "Don't even suggest such a thing to the universe, please and thank you."

She walked over to the bed and sank down a respectable distance away from me. "In two hours, we depart for a town tour. A tour of this town. Serenade Creek. Where we live. Where everyone knows us. Inside the Enchanted Rose Inn? Inside the happy love bubble? We could maybe convince the people who do not know me that we're a happy couple. But out there?" She gestured out the window. "Out there where everyone knows me as Cursed Bailey Can't Get a Man and you as Fort Knox?"

I laughed despite everything. "Fort Knox?"

She rolled her eyes. "C'mon. You know that's what everyone calls you."

"Everyone?" I raised a brow. "Even you?"

"I typically refer to you as Principal Knox or, you know..."

"Not at all," I finished for her.

"My point is," she deftly changed the subject. "We barely made it out of the lobby with our lies and our lives intact. On the streets of Serenade Creek? Nobody's gonna buy it. Our covers will be instantly blown."

Her voice trailed off.

She was right, once again.

"I'll get us out of it," I said, with more optimism about my odds than I actually felt.

But I had to try, because on the off chance our covers weren't instantly blown, that might be worse. With the way the Hearts & Charts Brigade was watching me and all of the rumors currently swirling about her, for Bailey's sake, I didn't want to risk setting off any speculation that she and I were... anything.

CHAPTER SIX

As soon as Knox left the room, I did a couple of quick yoga poses to try to get some of the tension out of my body. If I didn't, by the time Luke and Jessa were husband and wife, my shoulders would be able to double as earmuffs.

Instead of focusing on my breathing, I focused on the clock.

The only meditating I did was on two sentences, which I repeated in my head like the world's least relaxing mantra:

I yeeted a quarter into the Fountain of Forever.

Two minutes later, I became Knox's fake girlfriend.

Did it mean...

I scoffed.

Of course it didn't.

All it meant was that I was in the wrong place at the wrong time and then, immediately thereafter, in an even more wrong place at an even more wrong time.

It absolutely, positively did not mean that the universe

heard my accidental cry of readiness and ushered my soul mate right out of one of the Enchanted Rose Inn's side entrances.

I rolled my neck a few times and went back to the window seat. I didn't see my cardinal—*do not think of it as your cardinal, Bailey, the thing is stalking you*—but I knew he was out there. He had been taunting me—*purdy purdy purdy*—while Knox and I talked.

I sat and pulled up my knees, hugging them to my chest.

Man, the universe had a twisted sense of humor and I was the butt of this joke.

The last time I'd played pretend, I'd told myself it was harmless.

Last July, bored and freshly bruised by my third Eternal Bouquet catch, I went to the Summer Lovin' Festival in disguise—wig, sunglasses, and a plan to blend in with the tourists.

I hadn't expected to meet anyone. But I had. Knox.

He was behind me in line for the Ferris wheel when the attendant asked if I was riding alone. "Yes," I answered, a little too enthusiastically.

"Aww, where's the fun in that? Double up with me," Knox said, like it was no big deal.

"Visiting?" I asked, already knowing the answer. He had a face you remembered.

"Here for the week."

"Me too."

The lie slipped out. Slipped out before I knew what I was saying. I hadn't intended to lie.

But once I'd said it... I hadn't been able to stop thinking... would it be so bad? To pretend to be a tourist in Serenade

Creek and spend it with this cute guy? To enjoy the festival without feeling pitiful and alone?

We said no last names, no socials, no real-life details. Just Bailey and Knox. One week of fun in the sun.

One week of pretending never hurt anyone, I'd told myself.

And now here I was. Almost a year later.

Telling myself that lie again, like I was caught in some terrible time loop movie.

One week of pretending never hurt anyone, I told myself.

And it was a lie, because, well, Knox had been in town that week interviewing to be the assistant principal at the elementary school where I taught art.

What a *cliche.*

I had gotten hurt.

I deserve one week of pretending, I'd told myself.

But I suppose the universe decided I deserved two.

The more I thought, the more my muscles tightened.

I glanced at the grandfather clock. Knox had been gone for twenty minutes.

My spine felt like a steel rod.

One quick Thread the Needle.

And of course, that's when Knox returned. When I was contorted on the floor.

"You okay down there?"

You couldn't have come back when I was sitting in the window seat looking like a pretty princess?

"Yup," I said, without looking up. "Did you get us out of the tour?"

"Well, at first she kind of short-circuited. Made this sound like a robot rebooting. Blinked rapidly," he said. Then he sighed. "She has no problem saying no. Maybe she could teach you how."

"Maybe she could teach *us* how, Mr. I Got Roped Into This," I corrected. I let out a breath and maneuvered, twisting to the other side, facing him, though from this angle, I mostly saw his feet and shins.

I pulled myself up into a sitting position. "What are you holding?"

He had it kind of tucked between his arm and his side but in a very obvious *I Don't Want You To See This* way.

"Two adult diapers," he said. How can someone look adorable saying those words? Shouldn't be possible but Knox made it so.

"Okay, this might be the point where I draw the line," I said, getting to my feet. "Why do you have two adult diapers?"

"Because Jessa gave them to me after I told her we couldn't go on the tour because we both have diarrhea."

I dropped my face into my hands. "Knox, Serenade Creek is embarrassing me enough right now, really. You do not have to play wingman."

Also: Why does Jessa have adult diapers on hand?

WE WERE BEING CHAUFFEURED around Serenade Creek in eight-seater golf carts: One for the bride and bridesmaids and one for the groom and groomsmen. While this meant I had to make small talk with a bunch of women who'd clearly known each other for years, I didn't mind because while Knox and I were separated I didn't have to worry if we looked lovey-dovey enough to fool the wedding party while also appearing platonic enough not to fall into any Hearts & Charts Brigade booby traps.

Jessa was a completely different person now than she had been in the Enchanted Rose lobby earlier. She grinned from ear to ear. There was a lightness about her—laid-back bordering on bubbly. And when she found something funny, she didn't just laugh—she guffawed and everyone else joined in as if it was contagious, until tears streamed down their faces. Inevitably one of them would snort and the laughter would begin anew. (Maybe that was the reason for the adult diapers?)

"Bailey," she said, linking arms with me as we gathered in front of Sunblush Orchards, the first stop on the tour. I'd been here hundreds, if not a thousand times. "I am so glad you're here! Knox said you've lived in Serenade Creek your entire life, so I expect the inside scoop on everything!"

"I think the guide will more than provide," I told her.

Unfortunately, the tour guide was Patty Lou Henderson. Well. Fortunate for Jessa: Patty Lou knew everything about Serenade Creek. Unfortunate for me and Knox, because—Patty Lou also made sure to pass along any juicy bits to everyone else in town.

"Well," Jessa said. "Anything she leaves out, you have to tell me later."

Her smile was genuine, showing off dimples in her cheeks. Her eyes twinkled. She looked like every bride should: Radiant with happiness. Glowing with joy.

And if I was playing even an itty bitty part in that happiness, that joy? Maybe this was the right thing to do. Maybe the ends would justify the means.

In a couple of months, Knox would tell her and Luke we amicably broke up and she would have amazing memories of this week. She'd never have to be the wiser.

"Oops," she said. "Looks like she's ready to get started!"

She gave me an impulsive kiss on the cheek and raced over to Luke, leaping into his arms, wrapping her legs around his waist, and burying her face in his neck. She squealed as he spun her around.

And I wished I didn't want that so bad.

I glanced away from them and my eyes met Knox's. He'd been standing next to Luke, but he sidled over to me.

"Everyone!" Patty Lou trilled. She was wearing a headset and a floppy hat and carried a clipboard. "You are really in for a treat here today! When I say Sunblush Orchards is one of a kind, I mean it. Let's walk and talk, shall we?"

Everyone fell into a ragged line behind her in twos and threes. I held back, wanting to be in the back of the pack, hoping Patty Lou wouldn't notice me.

"You okay?" Knox's fingers grazed my elbow.

"I'm fine," I said, because maybe I was and what if I wasn't? Then I sidestepped, putting some distance between us. "No touching, remember?"

I waited for him to say it was an accidental brushing of his hand against my arm but he didn't.

The orchard smelled like overripe fruit, warmed wood, and something faintly floral and nostalgic that made my stomach twist.

The trees weren't in neat rows. They leaned, lounged, sprawled like they'd grown tired of being polite and would rather spread out however they pleased. Some were blooming. Some were dropping fruit. Some were doing both like it was no big deal.

Beyond the orchard, the trees thickened across the sloping foothills of the Blue Ridge Mountains like they'd been poured there from a can of hazy blue paint—splattered, moody and annoyingly beautiful.

"The orchard keeps its own time and the trees here bloom on their own time, yes, occasionally even out of season," Patty Lou said, her voice carrying all the way back to us. "And those who wander in often forget the hour—or what they came for. Proposals happen here without planning. Breakups happen without broken hearts. People come to pick apples and leave having spoken things they didn't mean to speak out loud."

I walked a few paces ahead of Knox, trying to look like I'd gotten caught up in taking in the sights and had accidentally drifted away from my beloved, trying not to breathe too deeply. The scent felt like it indeed might go straight to my head and make me say things I'd regret.

Every few feet, we passed another hand-lettered sign hanging from a branch: *Plumish Persuasion, Golden Pining, Cherry Cordial Confessions.*

"The trees in Sunblush are the oldest living things in the county. You'll find apples and peaches and pears and plums... some mixed on the same trees, and our local historians give their word that it's nature, not grafting."

The ground was soft, covered in a mix of moss and fallen petals, and the late afternoon sunlight filtering through the branches hit in uneven patches, casting gold against rose against shadow.

Suddenly Luke pushed past the two guys in front of me.

He fell into step with me, and Knox caught up to us, flanking my other side.

"What's up?" Knox asked.

"You have to sell this better," Luke told me, his voice low and exasperated. "You look like you think Knox smells bad."

Knox surreptitiously glimpsed down at his left armpit, the one furthest away from me, and sniffed.

Why, oh, why, was that endearing?

"I just—"

"I don't want her to think you all are fighting and about to break up and ruin the wedding. She's already suspicious because of the room thing," Luke said.

"Jess is fine," Knox said. "Listen. That's her laughing."

"Could you try to look obsessed with each other?" Luke asked, just on this side of begging.

Knox's brow furrowed. "No." He shook his head.

"Could you at least hold hands?" Luke tried again, and this time, yep, he slid right into begging territory.

Knox glanced sideways at me.

My heartbeat sped up at just the thought of holding his hand. Was I twelve?

"I'm not trying to be a spoilsport, but not all couples are into PDA," I said, as lightly as possible.

"I'm not trying to be a jerk, but not all couples are being paid to be a couple," Luke said.

"You *are* being a jerk, my dude," Knox said. "And I'm not being paid to do anything. My palms are sweaty and gross and I'm not going to subject Bailey to that. Go. Be with Jess. Have fun. Stop worrying so much."

Luke harrumphed, but parted the line again and headed back up front.

"You kind of said no," Knox said, with a half-grin.

I couldn't help myself. I half-grinned too. "I kind of did, didn't I?"

Purdy purdy purdy.

I snapped my head up.

But then I saw it.

A cardinal—though certainly it couldn't be the same cardinal, right?—perched on a crooked branch just ahead, his red feathers like a warning flare against the blush pink blossoms.

He tilted his head.

I glared at him. "Stop it."

"What was I doing?" Knox asked.

"I wasn't talking to you," I muttered...and that's when my foot caught on a twisted root hiding beneath a pile of fallen petals.

I stumbled forward, arms pinwheeling, certain I was going to bash into the groomsmen right in front of us and send everyone toppling like bowling pins. But then I grabbed onto something solid.... Knox's hand. His fingers, strong and warm, clasped mine.

Spoiler alert: His palms weren't sweaty at all.

For a second, all I could do was look at his thumb brushing over my knuckle, like it was the most natural thing in the world.

"What Luke wants, Luke gets, huh?" Knox asked.

And I realized why this fake dating thing was going to be so dangerous. It wasn't because Jessa might find out and drown us all in the creek. It was because when Knox Showalter held my hand, the no touching rule went out the window, because I simply forgot how to let go.

CHAPTER SEVEN

KNOX

"The tour was pretty cool, right?" Knox asked.

"Yeah," I said, though half of it was lost in a yawn.

It was midnight and the last time I'd sent him down to check, no one other than us had gone up to their suites yet.

I had abandoned the window seat about an hour ago and was curled up on the couch, my head on a throw pillow and a quilt over my legs, more for comfort than warmth. There had been twelve stops on the tour, then dinner here at the inn, which I would later tell Cherish, Addy, Kelsie, and Lyric all about, and make them more jealous than they'd ever been of anyone in their entire lives. But now, my eyelids were heavy and I was fighting a losing battle with sleep.

By the time I got home, it might be time to turn right around and come back.

Knox was sitting up in bed, reading.

"I'd never been to any of those places. Some of them I hadn't even heard of," he said.

But I smiled. "Well, you've only lived here a year and you've kind of got a reputation as a workaholic recluse."

He grinned at me over the top of his book. "Guilty as charged on both accounts."

We fell quiet for a minute, but I could feel him watching me.

"I'm glad it's you," he said.

I glanced over at him.

"I mean, instead of a stranger," he added.

I nodded and looked away again.

"You didn't eat any dessert tonight. And you didn't try any of the fruit at the orchard," he said.

"Are you keeping a food diary on my behalf, Mr. Showalter?"

"Nah. Just making conversation. And also wondering if maybe I could convince you to sneak into the kitchen with me and see if there's any of that fruit torte left because I could really go for seconds."

"It was good, huh?" I asked, and immediately wished I hadn't.

Of course it had been good, or else he wouldn't want seconds.

"Soooo good," he said, with a moan.

He apparently hadn't heard Patty Lou's spiel about the fruit during the walk through Sunblush Orchards. Or maybe she hadn't given it this time. But I knew it by heart.

They say if you walk the rows while holding hands, the orchard will know if it's right. If it is, the fruit will taste sweeter than anything you've ever had. If it's not... it'll taste like ash and goodbyes.

We had walked the rows holding hands. I didn't want to know what the fruit tasted like.

It's just another silly Serenade Creek superstition.

"Sorry Jessa asked you how your diarrhea was in front of everyone."

I laughed, despite myself. "Well, to her credit, I don't think she intended for everyone to hear. The string quartet stopped playing at the most inopportune moment, is all."

I yawned again. "Do you think they'll go this late every night?"

"Well, Jessa will probably have everybody in bed by 6:00 p.m. the night before the wedding so no one has under-eye bags for the ceremony, but other than that? Eh... hard to say."

I tried not to sigh. What a plot twist. I'd spent my whole life wanting to get inside the Enchanted Rose Inn and now that I had the opportunity, I was wasting it by daydreaming about going home.

As if reading my thoughts, Knox said, "You could just stay here, you know. I'll take the couch."

"Maybe I'll just rest my eyes for a few minutes."

They were already closing.

"Do you want me to..."

Knox was still speaking but his voice sounded so far away.

"Mm-mmm," I murmured, rolling over onto my side, pressing my face into the velvety cushions.

When I opened my eyes again, sun streamed into the room.

And I was... in the bed.

What was this mattress made of? Magic and clouds?

I sat up and stretched.

I had never felt so well-rested.

I glanced around. In the morning light, everything in the room from the lamps to the furniture seemed to shimmer.

Knox was on the couch now. Well, mostly on the couch. One of his legs, bent at the knee, hung off it, a bare foot on the floor.

Obviously, I had to wake him up. The alternative was that I was likely going to get caught watching him sleep. And, yeah, not happening.

I picked up one of the many pillows and tossed it at him.

He groaned. "Whaaaaaaaaaaatisssittt?"

I almost giggled. Contrary to what seeing him friendly and personable in the school hallways at 6:45 a.m. might have led me to believe: Knox Showalter was not a morning person. He sounded downright cranky. It was kind of cute.

Cracking one eye opened, he peered at me. "Did you throw something at me?"

"Did you move me?" I asked. "Because picking me up, carrying me to bed, and tucking me in probably breaks our no-touching rule in about nine ways."

"I didn't carry you. You just kind of levitated over there," he flopped his hand around in a gesture that I guess was supposed to represent levitating.

"For future reference, *hey, you sleepwalked* might be a bit more believable."

"Well, it's Serenade Creek. We don't do believable. We do magic."

He was staring at me through both eyes now, but they were half-open, at best. "What time is it?"

"I dunno. Light."

"Light isn't a time. It's a... state of not darkness."

I laughed. "You're one of those people who needs six

cups of coffee before you can stand upright without assistance, aren't you?"

"No, I just need to wake up naturally or else..." he mumbled something about circadian rhythms and death.

I grabbed my phone.

"It's only 6:15. Certainly everyone won't be up and at 'em too early after the late night last night," I said, realizing I didn't even know when everyone finally went to bed. "Do you want to go back to sleep for a while?"

"Umph."

"I'm going to take that as a yes," I said, getting out of bed, still wearing the clothes I'd worn yesterday. "Do you mind if I take a shower?"

"Please do," he said.

"Since I'm not sure you're actually conscious, I won't take offense at that."

As I walked past the couch, I was very tempted to reach down and ruffle his hair, but I resisted. I stuck my phone in my pocket and retrieved the things I'd need from my duffel so I wouldn't have to lug it in the bathroom with me.

While I was waiting on the tub to fill—having changed my mind about the shower immediately upon spying a bottle of the inn's own Enchanted Rose bubble bath—I checked my texts. They were mostly from Cherish asking how it was going, if the fountain had done its thing, if Jessa was buying me and Knox as a couple, begging me not to blow our cover, and a sad selfie of herself alone in a booth at the Honey & Thyme Cafe. She must have decided to go to lunch with her father, after all—and got stood up, as predicted.

I messaged her back and then settled in for a nice, luxurious soak.

As a teacher—unless you count that last day of school

when I let both my mind and my students go a little feral—I'd gotten pretty good at compartmentalizing. Leaving my personal bad moods and grievances outside of my classroom was important.

I'd used that skill yesterday, keeping certain things out of my mind.

But now, those thoughts were front and center, and demanding to be processed.

I don't know how you found the key to unlock his heart, but...

That frozen heart of yours has melted, hasn't it?

You did the impossible, girlie. I didn't think he'd ever find love again. You must be something really special.

Things Jessa had said about Knox yesterday, right after we met.

And now, I couldn't help but wonder: Did Knox have some tragic romantic history I didn't know about?

Since I had not, in fact, melted anything or found a key, was his heart still frozen or locked up tight?

What don't I know about you, Knox?

And whatever your secrets are, are they why you didn't want me?

My goodness.

Cursed as I may or may not be, I am not going to be that girl.

My fingers pruney and the water tepid, I decided it was time to dry off and face the day—whatever that may entail.

I hadn't paid attention to whether or not there was a dress code included in the itinerary and had no idea what kind of attire would be most appropriate for today's mystery events. That's why my duffel had been so heavy—I wanted to make sure I had something right to wear for every occasion, so I'd practically packed my whole closet and half of my dresser drawers. I was going with an outfit I felt comfortable in for now—I could always change later.

I'd just buttoned my favorite pair of paper bag shorts when I heard voices outside the bathroom door. I pulled my linen tank over my head and pressed my ear against the door.

"Knox Showalter, did you sleep on the couch, and why?"

Jessa.

Oh, no.

"Why did you just burst into my... our... our room without knocking?"

"Whoa. I knocked eight times and then I convinced the owners that y'all might be dead in here from a gas leak or something and got the master key."

"Twenty-four hours in the south and you're already saying *y'all* like you've lived here your whole life."

"Knoxxy. Why did you sleep on the couch? Stop deflecting, grumpypants."

If she found out we weren't sharing the bed, Jessa's house-of-cards belief in our True Love would come crashing down. No way was Knox alert enough to come up with a believable cover story.

I flung the door open and rushed out into the suite.

"Jessa!" I said, feigning surprise in a way I hope sounded legit. "Oh, my gosh! It's a good thing I didn't come out here buck naked, isn't it!"

Knox was sitting up, the quilt wrapped around his shoulders. It was obvious he'd been sleeping on the couch. I plopped down beside him, getting all up in his space. I leaned into him, resting my head on his shoulder.

"Did you finally wake up, baby?" I rubbed his knee... his bare knee...

He'd been all covered up when I went to the bathroom, but apparently, he'd slept in boxer shorts. Just boxer shorts.

Do not ogle his chest. I repeat: Do not ogle his chest.

I moved my hand up to a safe zone and playfully pinched his cheek. Then I grinned at Jessa, keeping my eyes glued to her. "I had to kick him out of bed around 2:00 a.m. because he was snoring so loud I'm surprised y'all couldn't hear him in your room."

"We're on the first floor," she said.

"I know," I replied.

"We're going to get you some of those strips for your nose," Jessa told him.

"I don't need nose strips," he said.

"Well, I bet Bailey's gonna disagree, because we're spending the day hiking, and the night camping, and the two of you are going to be sharing a tent about the size of that bed!" She clapped her hands together and it sounded like thunder in my head. "Now get dressed and let's goooooooo. Be downstairs in twenty minutes or I'm coming back up here and I'm bringing reinforcements."

"Did she say...?" Knox asked.

"Yep."

"Did you call me baby?"

"Yep again," I said, realizing that not only had I called him baby, it had slipped out naturally.

My simple rules were proving hard to follow already.

CHAPTER EIGHT

BAILEY

The fifteen-passenger van smelled like bug spray and kettle corn, and I was fairly certain my left leg had gone numb somewhere around mile two.

Luke was driving. Jessa rode shotgun. I was the last to climb in, by design, and tried to sit in the very back seat with Melody, the maid of questionable honor (as she referred to herself) but Jessa caught sight of it in the rear view mirror and made everyone get back out so she could rearrange the twelve of us—five bridesmaids, five groomsmen—like human Tetris pieces until I was tucked neatly against Knox's side.

I tried to pay attention to everyone but him. I was going to be spending a week with these people, so the best thing I could do for myself—and for Jessa—was to try to fit in, and I had to start by getting to know everyone. So far I'd learned that Michael seemed to be obsessed with fun facts and Rafe seemed to think everything could be a competition. But the chatter didn't last long before Jessa blared a playlist called

"Campfire Kiss Vibes" and I channeled all my focus into not accidentally resting my head on Knox's shoulder.

He hadn't said much since we hit the road. Just a quiet "Hey," when I slid into the seat beside him, followed by a murmured, "You okay?"

I nodded. I would try to be okay. Because I had to. But I wasn't there, not yet.

Now Knox and I stayed quiet while the rest of the van sang along with the carefully curated tunes. Possibly because they were afraid Jessa would yell at them if they didn't. She seemed to oscillate pretty wildly between Blissful Bride and Bridezilla without much notice. Weddings are stressful and I imagined it was taking all the strength she had just to not let the recent falling out with one of her best friends ruin it all. I couldn't imagine losing Cherish or Addy or Lyric or Kels.

I didn't have the heart to belt out love songs, but I bobbed my head and lip synced now and then to pass the vibe check if she happened to glance back.

Now Knox leaned in.

"Is this worse or better than 100 Bottles of Beer?" he whispered as Rick Astley's "Never Gonna Give You Up" kicked into the chorus. Everyone was shouting out the lyrics and dancing in their seats. Everyone but us, anyway.

"Do not give them any ideas," I whispered back, with a laugh.

"We're almost there!" Jessa called out from the passenger seat, turning the music way down to be heard. "You guys are gonna love it. There are fireflies and some of the country's best stargazing and a creek that may or may not be magical."

"Define magical," Luke said.

"Well, for starters, the water sounds like it's singing a lullaby, hence the name Serenade Creek. But, but, but... the best part! You toss a rock in and ask for something you want and sometimes the water tosses the rock back. That's how you know your wish has been granted."

Knox glanced at me, brows raised, as if asking for confirmation or denial.

I shrugged, because yeah, I used to believe, but now—that was just one of many Serenade Creek superstitions. I'd never seen the creek toss a rock back, nor did I know anyone who had. Sure, everyone knew someone who knew someone who'd supposedly witnessed the magic, which is how it always was with these things. I didn't want to be a buzzkill, though. If Jessa wanted to believe, I'd let her believe.

When we pulled into the parking lot, but before everyone could even pile out of the van, Jessa was whistling for our attention.

"She's got a clipboard," Knox said to me out of the side of his mouth, like a cartoon character trying to be covert, but loud enough for Jessa to hear. "That can't be a good thing."

"Yes, Knox, I do have a clipboard." She waved it in the air. "It's for keeping score. As you all know, many of our activities this week are rooted in things Luke and I both loved to do when we were growing up. We both went to summer camps and loved the experiences so today we're going to have a ten-event competition that the camp I used to go to, Camp Wishaway, kicked off each season with. They called it something hokey, but I'm calling it the Decathlon of Destiny. The events will take place throughout the day and tonight, we'll crown first, second, and third place."

"Did she say decathlon?" Knox whispered.

"What do the winners get?" Rafe asked.

Jessa didn't miss a beat. "My good graces and a dollar store trophy!"

"Can we sit out, though?" Greer squinted into the sun and Corey? Rory? took off his sunglasses and perched them on her face. Aww. "Don't touch me, you goon," she smacked him lightly across the chest. Well. It was almost a sweet moment. "My ankle's feeling funky, J."

"Only with a doctor's note," Jessa said. "Now, let's pair you all up. Honey, you ready?"

"Yes," Luke said and that was when I noticed what he was holding. Strips of cloth.

"Is he going to blindfold us or..." I whispered to Knox.

"I mean, I think it's either that or he's on standby to make tourniquets. If bows and arrows come out next, we make a run for it, okay?"

My lips twitched.

"Knox and Bailey, obviously," Jessa said.

Obviously.

"Melody and Blain."

They both groaned, then made offended faces at each other. I hid my laugh behind my hand.

"Whoa, what are you doing there, bud?" Knox asked as Luke strode over to us and crouched down, grabbing Knox's shin.

"The first event is a three-legged race to the campsite."

Wait, what?

"Lucas!" Jessa cried. "Spoiler alert."

"Well, sweetums, I can't really bind people's legs together without them knowing. Hey, Bailey, can you step a little bit closer to Knox?"

No. No, I absolutely cannot.

But I did, and Luke tied mine and Knox's ankles together while I plotted ways I was absolutely going to make Cherish pay for this. I did not agree to this level of skin-to-skin contact.

Do not look at him, do not look at him, do not look at him.

Melody had snatched a piece of the binding from Luke as he passed her. "I've got this," she said. "I was a Girl Scout for six months. I can make a slipknot. Or a love knot. Or a vengeance knot. One sec."

"Should I be worried that you know what a vengeance knot is?" Blain asked.

"Only if you slow me down."

"The way to win this," Faye was saying to Michael as my soul slowly left my body because why on earth does Knox Showalter smell so good when I am literally attached to him, "is to channel harmony and move as one body."

"Or, hear me out," Michael said. "We could just hop like lunatics and pray we don't eat dirt."

"That sounds like a solid plan," Knox whispered and I could feel his breath on the side of my face.

"Teamwork and coordination, people! LET'S GO!" Rafe bellowed, as if we were all the varsity football team and he was our coach and this was the homecoming game.

"Should we link arms? I think maybe we should—"

"No." Greer shut Corey down without hesitation and with admirable efficiency. "I'd rather eat dirt."

"Campsite is that way!" Jessa pointed dramatically at the trailhead. "First pair there gets to skip unloading the van! Everyone else needs to come on back and grab all you can carry!"

The bridesmaids squealed. The groomsmen groaned.

"Are your feet gonna be okay?" Knox asked me, quietly. Like he was really my boyfriend, making sure I was taken care of down to my toes.

Before we'd left the Enchanted Rose, Jessa had presented all of the ladies with matching hiking boots, in Pink Reverie, one of her wedding colors. Mine were a size too small, having been meant for the bridesmaid I was replacing.

I nodded.

"I'm going to put my arm around your shoulders," Knox said. "And you put your arm around my waist."

"Okay," I said, and took a deep breath before complying.

I dreaded his touch. I craved his touch.

I was absolutely going to make Cherish pay.

"There we go," he said.

"Just run-walk normally and I'll match your pace," Knox said.

"AND GO!" Jessa yelled.

We stumbled forward, moving like we didn't want to keep a car waiting that had braked to let us cross a street. Awkward at first, but not as awkward as I expected.

"Left foot," Knox murmured.

I stepped with my left. So did he.

"Right."

We moved again, faster this time. My fingers were curled against the edge of his T-shirt, barely holding on, trying not to register the warmth of his body.

A few yards in, I realized something shocking.

We weren't terrible.

In fact, we were... good?

"Oh my gosh," I whispered. "Are we accidentally athletic?"

Knox laughed. "I wouldn't go that far, but let's not jinx it."

Behind us, someone shrieked—Melody, I thought. Rafe

yelled "GO! GO! GO! PUSH THROUGH THE PAIN!" like this was the Olympics. Either a hyena had joined us or Greer was having some sort of laughing fit.

I focused on our stride. Step. Step. Don't overthink it. Don't fall.

My grip on him tightened.

He was solid. Steady. The kind of person who said he'd match your pace and meant it.

"We're actually doing it," I breathed.

"Of course we are." His voice was low and sure.

The finish line—marked by a paper sign that read *Happily Ever After or Bust*—was just ahead.

"Let's finish strong," he said.

"Copy that."

We surged forward. Our rhythm perfect. A final sprint.

When we crossed the invisible line and stopped, I realized two things at once: We'd won. And I really didn't want to let him go.

This was not good.

He leaned down to untie us as the others stumbled towards us in a clump.

"Good job, partner," he said, holding out his fist for me to bump.

I tapped it lightly with mine. "Yeah."

"I know we technically don't have to since we won, but should we help the others unload the van?" he asked.

Ordinarily, this would raise my hackles. Someone tossing responsibility that wasn't mine at me. But I sensed that wasn't what Knox was trying to do. He was letting me off the hook from being alone, here, with him while everyone else went back.

"Yeah. Let's."

When all the gear had been brought to the campsite, Jessa clapped her hands. "Tents up, then lunch! There are mason jar salads and customized trail mix and strawberry tea. We'll have s'mores tonight, obviously."

"And ghost stories," Luke said, coming up behind her and wrapping his arms around her waist. "Booooooo."

She elbowed him playfully, but turned to face him, standing on her tiptoes and kissing him in a way that made someone shout, "Get a tent, you two!"

I set my backpack down on a patch of grass. Knox stepped up beside me.

"You know how to pitch a tent?" he asked.

"Nope. But I guess we can fake it like everything else, huh?"

He emptied out our tent bag. We crouched beside the mess of nylon and poles, and I tried to focus on the logistics. Slide this through there. Snap that into place. Do not think about how close he was now or, worse, the fact that tonight, we'd be inside this thing together, even closer.

His knuckles brushed mine when we reached for the same stake, and neither of us pulled back fast enough to make it casual.

"Sorry," he said softly.

"It's okay," I murmured.

When we were done, I stepped back and stared at it. Then at Knox.

It was *tiny*.

"A body bag built for two, yay," I murmured.

"Let's go eat," he said. He pointed at a hammock hung between two tulip poplars. "I can always sleep in that to give you some space. Jessa never gave me those nose strips so I can tell her you kicked me out of the tent when I started snoring."

"Sure, because I'm not even your real girlfriend, but our lack of intimacy is my fault."

Oh. My. Goodness.

It slipped out.

"Well," he said, shifting from foot to foot. "Technically only my nasal passages are to blame."

"I have never craved a mason jar salad more in my life," I said, brushing past him. "Excuse me."

The others were already digging into lunch, which was set up on a collection of picnic blankets beneath the trees. I sat cross-legged, piercing pieces of lettuce with my fork but never actually consuming any, while Knox sprawled beside me, elbow grazing my knee every time he reached for something.

"So," Jessa said. "I realized last night, I don't even know how you two met—"

"She realized that at three in the morning and woke me up to tell me so," Luke said, but he winked at her to show he was teasing and not bothered at all.

And everyone was looking at me, expectantly.

"Tell us everything, Bailey!" Jessa cried.

I opened my mouth. "Uh—"

Knox's gaze was on my face like a caress.

"Don't put her on the spot, Jessa. She's not here to give a Ted Talk."

"Awww, come on," one of the other bridesmaids, Greer, said. "We all wanna know what sorcery this one," she gestured at me, "worked on Mr. Never Gonna Love Again."

Mr. Never Gonna Love Again.

"Greer," Luke said. There was a warning in his tone that made me do a double take.

"It was last June," Knox said.

He said it so simply, so flatly, like he was reading it off a form. But then he added, "It was at the Summer Lovin' Festival," and something shifted in his voice.

"Why were you at a *Summer Lovin'* Festival?" one of the guys, Blain, scoffed.

"Because fried food, obviously," another guy—Corey? I think it's Corey, not Rory—laughed.

"Yes, everyone knows I cannot resist a funnel cake," Knox said.

I pushed away the memory of him brushing powdered sugar from a funnel cake off the tip of my nose. We'd split one every day.

"Awww," Jessa said, scooting closer. "Let me guess. Our girl Bailey wanted to enter the kissing contest but the loser she was on a date with got food poisoning—from the funnel cakes—and she said, 'Hey, hottie, wanna smooch?' and you said, 'No, not now. I need a funnel cake.' And she said 'Nooooo, you absolutely cannot!' and saved you from severe gastrointestinal distress and in return you..."

She made a smooching face.

Wow, the imagination is strong with this one. Also, she'd done her research. There was a kissing contest every year to kick off the festival, but I'd pretty much rather die than participate.

"No," Knox said, with a faint smile. "We met at the Ferris wheel. She was in front of me in line, alone. The ride operator asked if she was flying solo, and I—I don't know. I just said, 'Double up with me.'"

He glanced over at me, like he wasn't sure how much to say.

"Okay but that's adorable," Jessa's eyes sparkled. "You literally swept her off her feet."

Accurate. So accurate.

She was looking at me so I forced a grin.

"We spent that whole week together," he continued, and his voice was too soft now. Too real. "Rode everything two, three times. Made some unfortunate culinary choices. Danced under lights that looked like stars and didn't care who was watching."

A breath hitched in my throat.

"I don't think I've ever laughed that much in one week," he said. "Or felt that... free."

There was a moment of silence. The group had gone still.

He added, quietly, "It was the best time. I can't remember having more fun. Ever."

Everyone let out some version of *awww*. A dreamy sigh. A squeal.

"Yeah," I said softly. "It was a great week."

His eyes met mine. He tilted his head. I wondered if he remembered the words as his own. If he realized I was only parroting back what he'd once said to me.

Jessa beamed. "Aww, and by the time the week was up, you were in love and you've been together ever since!"

"Yep," Knox said.

But he wasn't looking at me now, because we both knew that wasn't how it had happened at all.

Jessa lightly socked him in the shoulder. "I can't believe you've been in a relationship for almost a year and none of us knew." Then she said to Luke, "Babe, I am so glad we're going to be here for the kickoff of the Summer Lovin' Festival. What a perfect time to get married!"

"Married!" half the girls echoed, singsong, while half the guys shrieked it too, faking high-pitched voices to mock them.

"The maturity of this group is shocking," Jessa said, but she was laughing.

Everyone was laughing.

Except me. I tried to keep a smile plastered on, but I could feel it crumbling.

Thinking about the alternate reality did something to me. No, thinking about the fact that he could so easily lie and say we were in love did something to me. I set down my salad and my fork. "Um, excuse me. I have to..."

Somehow I got to my feet.

As I quickly walked away, I realized my mistake a split second before Jessa said, "Oh, my gosh. Knox! She's upset! Stop looking stupid and go after her!"

He caught up with me too fast.

"I'm just going to the bathroom," I lied.

"I, uh, think the bathrooms are actually that way—"

"Knox. We're in the woods. The bathroom is anywhere one can squat." My ears burned. Could my filter please work around this man?

I kept walking. So did he.

"Luke must be thrilled—huh," I said, because, yeah, that filter had not kicked in yet. "You really sold that."

"Bailey." His fingers grazed my arm. "I was only trying to take the spotlight off you. I didn't mean to—"

"Take a week I literally just told you meant something to me, infuse it with made-up feels, and use it to make your friends believe we're a product of Serenade Creek's love magic?"

I turned around so I was standing in front of him, facing him. Arms crossed. Lips pressed together.

He looked at me as if I was a jigsaw puzzle with no edges. Then he pressed the pads of his fingers against his forehead like I was giving him a migraine.

Then he looked at me again, and this time, his expression was almost pained.

"I didn't... I... Jessa asked how we met. I should've been quicker on my feet. I should've come up with a completely fictional story, I guess. But..." he shrugged. "She asked you how we met and I wanted to take the pressure off you, so I told her how we met. But I did not infuse any *made-up feels*."

"It was the best time, you said. I can't remember having more fun, you said. Ever?" I repeated his words with a pointed question mark at the end.

"Unequivocally true," he said.

Purdy purdy purdy.

At the sound, I glanced up. Sunlight filtered through the leaves in scattered golds and greens. No red anywhere in sight.

Not now, Mr. Cardinal.

"Then why..." I swallowed the rest of my sentence, even though the withheld words burned the back of my throat.

Do not be that girl, Bailey. Don't.

"Then why did it only have to be a week, Knox? Really?"

"Because that was what we initially agreed to—"

"No," I shook my head, and really, is there anything more pathetic than asking someone you want why they don't want you back? No. No, there is not. And if we hadn't been thrown together for Jessa and Luke's wedding, I never would've asked. But here we were. "I don't mean what we initially agreed to, when we first met, and I thought you were only going to be in Serenade Creek for a week and you thought I was only going to be in Serenade Creek for a week. I don't mean when we thought a week was all we could have. I mean when we realized there could be more and you decided you didn't want it."

Not when he was a cute, kind, funny guy I spent a week having fun with.

But when he was suddenly my boss, standing in my classroom, shifting from foot to foot, and saying, *It was a great week, but we kind of need to let what happened at the Summer Lovin' Festival stay at the Summer Lovin' Festival, huh?*

"We decided," he corrected.

I swallowed hard. Shook my head.

"Nope," I said, lightly. "You decided. I agreed. Because that's what Bailey Cooper does. She nods and says, yes, that's reasonable. Sounds good to me."

I shrugged. Angry at him. Angry at myself.

Why couldn't I just let it go? We spent a week together, for goodness' sake. It was nothing. A blip.

"Bailey," he said.

Aww, and by the time the week was up, you were in love and you've been together ever since!

That's what Jessa had said.

And perhaps that's why I couldn't let it go. Because by the time that week was up, I had been in love with Knox. In love with him and sure I'd never see him again.

But then everything had changed...

And for a moment, a moment, I dared to think...

For a split second, I believed...

Then he slammed the door on it.

I blinked.

"I think I hear Jessa calling us," I said though, no, I did not. "Why don't you head on back? I'll just... do what I came to do and then I'll meet you there."

He raked his bottom lip through his teeth, eyeing me with uncertainty.

"I promise I'm not going to walk back to town or hurl any rocks in the creek and wish things were different. I..."

Make it clear to him you have not been pining over him!

Do not say another word or it'll look like you're protesting too much and you're telling him you haven't been pining over him because you absolutely have been pining over him.

"Go," I said. "It's fine. I'm fine. You're fine. We're fine. We just need to make sure Jessa stays fine or this was all for nothing. Let's do what we need to do and then... we'll just go back to the way things were. Cordial professionalism with a hint of secret backstory."

He watched me for a second, like he was seeing more than I wanted to show.

Why on earth did he *look* at me like that?

A breeze blew through, as if nature was saying, Let's sweep some of this tension out of here.

My hair lifted off the back of my neck and settled again around my shoulders.

"Okay," Knox said, taking a few backward steps. "Okay."

Finally, he turned and headed back down the trail.

Purdy purdy purdy.

I snapped my gaze up again and this time saw the subdued, orange-ish red of a female cardinal obscured by the long, green needles on the branch of an Eastern hemlock.

Well, at least it wasn't the male cardinal that had been stalking me. That was good.

Unless... maybe he just took the day off and she was his sub?

"You're losing it, Bailey," I muttered, catching the cardinal's attention.

Her knowing black eyes landed on me.

"Shoo!" I said.

And as if she understood what the word meant, she flapped her wings and took flight, going in the same direction Knox had gone, as if following the trail.

CHAPTER NINE

KNOX

It was the middle of the night.

I'd guess it was around 2:00 a.m., but I didn't know for sure.

I was lying flat on my back, hands tucked beneath my head so I wouldn't accidentally touch Bailey, which had seemed like a perfectly sound plan at the time but now if I so much as shifted, she would end up with my elbow in her eye.

My plans to spend the night in the hammock had gone awry, since Jessa had called dibs while we were toasting marshmallows. *Let's sleep under the stars, baby. It'll be so romantic.*

Very romantic when we both end up on the ground covered in mosquito bites, Luke groused, but within minutes, he agreed. He wanted so badly to make her happy.

I wasn't going to be the guy to tell him that no matter what you did, sometimes it wasn't enough.

Instead, I sent up a silent prayer. Please let him and Jessa work. Let them get their happily ever after. Let them make it down the aisle, at least, for goodness' sakes.

Words couldn't express how much I hated weddings.

The night was still and quiet, except for the requisite crickets chirping and even they seemed to be keeping things at a respectful volume.

It was almost too quiet.

I was never going to be able to sleep. I wasn't a high-maintenance guy, but if I didn't want to be a zombie in the mornings, I really needed my white noise machine. Otherwise, my thoughts get too loud.

"Knox."

Careful not to jab her, I glanced at Bailey. Were my thoughts so loud that they'd woken her up?

"Hmm?" I asked.

She didn't respond.

Her eyes were still closed. Her sleeping bag rising and falling with her even breaths.

But I know I heard her say my name.

"Knox..."

It was her. Her lips were moving.

She shifted.

"What is it, Bailey?" I whispered.

No response.

"I buffem hussit. Buffem, buffem hussit."

Not even sure Google Translate could decipher that.

She was talking in her sleep.

She looked so vulnerable, caught in a moment no one was meant to witness. I should've looked away. I couldn't.

"Buffem hussit, Knox."

I smiled despite myself.

What are you trying to say to me, Bailey Cooper?

I hoped she was having sweet dreams, though I certainly didn't deserve to star in them.

I let out a sigh so large and dramatic the tent walls billowed.

Bailey shifted again, mumbling something unintelligible, then stilled.

GO TO SLEEP! I silently screamed at myself.

But my thoughts were already racing, rewinding through every moment of the day and Jessa's Decathlon of Destiny.

Bailey was relentless. Unapologetically competitive. And utterly, stupidly radiant.

It shouldn't have surprised me, after all I'd seen firsthand how seriously she took carnival games at the Summer Lovin' Festival. How her entire face would light up when she nailed a ring toss or hit the target at the dunk tank.

I remembered saying, "You should maybe consider letting me win something."

She'd scoffed, "I am possibly the world's biggest people pleaser. My worst trait is my tendency to say yes when I mean no. But... I would never say yes to someone asking me to let them win. I will share the stuffed animals I win with you, though."

Today she dragged us—*dragged me*—through every event like we were training for the Love Olympics. She even trash-talked the other teams, and somehow made it charming, made everyone laugh. She was quick, clever, locked in—and, heavens help me, kind of terrifying with a water balloon in her hand.

I chuckled, thinking about the final event, the wheelbarrow race.

I was the wheelbarrow. I am *thirty-three years old* and almost snapped my own wrist trying to keep up with her pace. My arms were shaking, my knees were screaming, and she just shouted "FASTER, SHOWALTER!" like she was leading a military drill and faster I went. Bailey Cooper, commander of the Decathlon of Destiny.

We crossed the finish line first.

And the way she laughed—head thrown back, joyous, alive—made me forget every single thing that had ever hurt.

Jessa handed her the dollar store trophy like it was the Stanley Cup, and Bailey held it up in the air and screamed, "VICTORY IS OURS!" Then she launched herself into my arms. Legs around my waist. Arms looped around my neck. Like we were the real deal. Like she couldn't help herself.

It only lasted a moment, but I can still feel the echo of it now. Her legs around me. Her laugh in my ear. Her breath against my neck.

Over her shoulder, I'd met Luke's gaze. He flashed me a covert thumbs up.

She was doing good. We were doing good.

But the thing was: I hadn't been pretending.

Okay, yeah, we were both pretending in as far as we weren't actually in a relationship. We hadn't been together for the past year.

But the smiling part? The laughing part? The having so much freaking fun it should kind of be illegal part?

All of that was real.

But the tightrope I was walking—making Jessa believe we were, indeed, the real deal while not hurting Bailey any more than I already had—was growing more precarious by the minute. And we were only going into day three. How was I going to keep my balance until Jessa and Luke said I do? And what if, when the week was up, I didn't want to go back to cordial professionalism with a hint of secret backstory?

No. It didn't matter what I wanted.

Again, as if she could hear what I was thinking, Bailey stirred.

Was she waking up?

No, I didn't think so.

But she did wriggle, obviously restless, before rolling over. Then rolling over again.

I inhaled and held my breath as she snuggled up against my side.

I should've moved her. Her face was nestled dangerously close to my armpit—a place no woman has ever willingly rested her cheek. But what really got me wasn't the unfortunate positioning. It was the ache that came from knowing I didn't deserve to hold her. We weren't really together. We couldn't be.

And sure, we'd sell the illusion for Jessa's sake. But there were lines I wasn't going to cross.

Not for Bailey's sake.

And not for mine.

But still, I didn't want to push her away.

And how would I extract myself without giving her a black eye by accidental elbowing?

Five minutes.

I'd give her five minutes to roll back over. If she didn't, I'd wake her up.

I'd just lie still and try not to sniff her hair like a creeper in the meantime. Unfortunately, I yawned and almost inhaled a few strands of it.

I should probably close my eyes so, in case she does wake up, she doesn't find me staring at her.

Yeah. Just five minutes.

The next time I opened my eyes, sunlight was slanting through the mesh panel of the tent and casting lines across Bailey's face.

I'd fallen asleep.

My arm was under her head. Her hand was resting on my chest. One of her knees was between mine.

I froze.

She looked... peaceful. Soft. Her features relaxed in a way I rarely saw when she was awake. Like the part of her that was always bracing for something had finally let go.

Then she stirred.

Her lashes fluttered. Her brows knit. Her body stiffened all at once like someone had flipped a switch.

I watched her eyes open, cautious and guarded, and she looked at me, but she didn't move away.

We laid there in silence for a moment, pretending the warmth between us didn't feel like something ancient and familiar.

Then she said, "Perhaps we're a bit too good at faking being a couple."

She moved her head. Her hand. Her knee.

And she scooted as far away from me as she could get.

"Bailey," I said, though I spit it out without any forethought, any planning. Any... anything.

"Mmm?" she muttered, then she yawned. From behind her hand, she said, "Mercy, I have morning breath. I should go brush my—"

"That week last summer meant something to me, too, Bailey," I said. "I had... feelings for you. And..."

Do not say they haven't completely gone away.

Don't you dare tell her that.

Her breath hitched, but she didn't look away. "And?"

"And... I just wanted you to know."

"Okay," she said. "Now I know."

We both stayed where we were. Eye contact maintained. Quiet and still.

Just let her go brush her teeth, dude.

But, no, my mouth kept moving and dumb words—potentially harmfully true words—kept falling out: "Do you know what my first thought was when I found out I got the job at Serenade Creek Elementary? When I decided to move to Serenade Creek?"

"The sensible thing to think would be, oh, I don't know, better practice ducking because the bouquets in that town are lethal—"

"Bailey. I'm serious."

She was bracing for what I was about to say next. I could see it. I could feel it.

"I thought, I can't wait until next summer. Maybe Bailey visits Serenade Creek every year and goes to the Summer Lovin' Festival. Maybe we'll get another week together. And then, I kind of spun this fantasy in my head, that maybe we could meet up every year and have a week together at the festival. One awesome week. Every year."

"I... I don't know what to say to that."

"Then I moved here. And found out you live here, too. And that... we were going to be working at the same school."

"And that's why we have to let what happened at the Summer Lovin' Festival stay at the Summer Lovin' Festival," she said. "Because you're my boss. I mean, that's how I think of you in my head. I mean... you may not be my direct supervisor, but you are above me on the hierarchy and you do have some authority over me."

She was adorable when she got flustered.

But suddenly her expression soured.

"That's it, right? We can't date because it wouldn't be appropriate, because of our jobs? That's all?"

I swallowed.

She looked at me expectantly, like if I dared to agree with her, she'd pounce on me and pin me down and tell me what a bald-faced liar I was.

Okay. Maybe not the pouncing and pinning me down part. But definitely the rest of it.

"Bay."

"Don't call me Bay, okay? We're colleagues, not friends, right?"

"Bailey."

"A friend would tell me the truth. I get that you don't wanna be my boyfriend, Knox. But... you can't even tell me the truth? Because I don't believe it has anything to do with your job or mine. I don't."

But the truth was a thousand razor blades I feared would cover both of us with tiny cuts.

"I can't date you. I just can't. And that is the truth."

"I'm gonna go brush my teeth and wash my face," she said.

I sat up. "Bailey—"

She didn't look back. "It's fine, Knox. Really."

She ducked out of the tent before I could say anything else.

Alone in the tent, I sank onto my sleeping bag, rubbed my palms over my face, and let out a breath that felt like it'd been trapped inside me for months.

It wasn't because she was a teacher at the school where I was the assistant principal. Though if it did happen, we'd both need to disclose it to Mr. Grogs, the principal. Luckily, there was no formal anti-fraternization policy in place, so... it wasn't like it was technically against any rules. It might be awkward but it wasn't out of the question.

But that's the excuse I'd given, because that's the one that made sense. The one that most people would accept without asking follow-up questions.

It's easier to say, "I'm your boss" than it is to say, "I'm broken in ways you don't know yet."

It's a heck of a lot easier than saying, *Bailey, I did want more time with you. I do want more time with you. I wanted a week every summer for the rest of forever with you, because a week at a time is all I can do. It's all I could risk. It's all I can risk.*

I pressed the heels of my hands to my eyes, and all I could see was her. Spinning in the festival lights last July, her hair catching the glow like it was a halo.

I knew she thought I didn't want her. That my excuses had just been the easy way out, to soften that blow.

But it would only hurt her more if I told her the truth. I did want her. I wanted her in a way I hadn't wanted anyone in a... long time.

I wanted her last summer. And I wanted her still.

But it didn't change anything.

CHAPTER TEN

BAILEY

After two nights roughing it—and thankfully on the second night, Knox did sleep in the hammock—we were back at the Enchanted Rose Inn.

I was halfway through twisting a ribbon around a lavender stem when I heard Jessa's voice—excited, delighted, and a little too close to manic.

"Oh my gosh, this is going to be EPIC! Where is Bailey?"

I froze. My fingers tightened around the ribbon like it was a lifeline. There were very few instances I could remember that started out with me hearing *Where is Bailey?* and subsequently ended in my favor.

Also: She knew where I was, in my assigned seat at the Bagels & Bouquets Brunch, and yes, I simultaneously developed a twitch at the word bouquets and began bargaining fervently with the good Lord above that the word bouquets was just thrown in to be alliterative and cute and there would not actually be any literal bouquets involved.

But no such luck. We were all making bouquets and Jessa would decide her favorite, which the florist would then use as inspiration in their design for the official bridesmaid bouquets.

Jessa plopped down beside me at the picnic table. Clipboard in one hand, champagne flute of Enchanted Rosé in the other. Her T-shirt said *Bride Vibes* and her aura said *chaotic neutral with a side of glitter.*

"Bailey," she said, eyes shining, "I just did something and you're going to love me forever."

"You've already got Luke on the hook forever, Jessa... do you really need me there, too?" I teased, but underneath the lightness in my voice, I was bracing myself for whatever she was about to throw at me. Hopefully it wouldn't be a bouquet.

"Ha ha," she said, but then: "Yes. Yes, I actually do."

I took a sip of my own Enchanted Rosé, which was not, in fact, rosé at all, but some kind of non-alcoholic punch that tasted like heaven or pure sugar, depending on who you asked. I, for one, loved it, but Maid of Dishonor Melody was sure that, after taking a couple of sips, she heard a plink and glanced down half-expecting to see one of her teeth had fallen out in protest and was floating in the glass. Apparently, the plink had been a confused bumblebee.

That stuff is sa-weeeeeeeeeeeeeeeeeeeeeeeeet, she'd said, made a face, and left to go see if she could find something to drink that wouldn't cause cavities to instantly form.

"You and Knox," Jessa said in a low voice, leaning forward conspiratorially, with a gleam I definitely did not like in her eyes, "are officially entered in the Summer Lovin' Kissing Contest Kickoff!"

I clutched the flowers in my hand so hard I really think I

heard a yelp of protest from the petals. "I'm sorry, we're what now?"

"You're entered!" she chirped. "Isn't that perfect? You guys are already Serenade Creek's cutest couple. This is fate."

I was going to barf. I was going to pass out. I was going to barf, then pass out in it.

"No, no. I think this was all *you*," I said. "No fate. All Jessa. And Jessa, I—"

"No!" She waved a dismissive hand and, yep, I still hate when people do that. "I don't mean it's fate in the woo-woo way, but fate in that I really need the grand prize and, yay, I have you and Knox—shoo-ins—to win it for me. Everyone saw your chemistry during the Decathlon of Destiny. You're going to crush this."

I tried to swallow down the panic, but nope, I'm afraid it's going to make an appearance, and it's bringing the three Enchanted Rosés I'd imbibed with it.

"I..." And that's all I had.

Say you can't!

But it felt like kicking a puppy.

"Bailey. Bailey. Bailey." Jessa wrapped her fingers around my wrist.

Oh, dear me. This woman was actually vibrating with giddiness or hopefulness or something else that was going to make it impossible for me to say no.

But I had to.

I could not kiss Knox in front of all of Serenade Creek.

I couldn't kiss Knox, period.

I couldn't even let myself remember what it was like to kiss Knox.

"Bailey," Jessa said again. "The two winners and ten of

their friends get to ride in the hot air balloon parade. That's literally the *entire* bridal party. It's like destiny planned it."

Then destiny hates me more than I thought she did.

I opened my mouth again. Object, Bailey. Say something reasonable, Bailey. Something like, "We're really sloppy kissers, for real, we won't win you anything, we'll just gross everyone out," or, "I have a tragic bouquet trauma that doesn't allow me to draw attention to myself in public right now."

But Jessa was looking at me with that face. That expression everyone has a version of.

The one that says, *Please do this for me, because if you don't, it will actually break my heart.*

Ugggggggggggh.

I glanced around.

Where are you, Knox? Come save me, Knox. Come save us, Knox.

But he was nowhere to be seen.

I looked up at the sky...just as that flipping cardinal flew overhead.

Don't you have somewhere else to be, dude?

"I will get on my knees and beg you," Jessa warned.

"She 100% will," Melody said.

"Jessa, please don't—"

"Please, please, please. Pretty please?" She clasped her hands together and batted her eyelashes at me.

"Do it, do it, do it," Greer began chanting, with Melody and Faye joining in.

I could already feel myself unraveling.

She took my silence as victory.

"I mean, I'd do it myself, obviously," she said, "but Luke's got that cough and I'm not risking mucus on my wedding day. If he gets me sick, I will seriously marry him and then kill him in the same twenty-four hours."

We'd already heard about Luke's cough and Jessa's fear of matrimonial mucus multiple times this morning.

"'Til death do you part' with efficiency," I muttered.

She beamed. "So, you're doing it!"

"I—"

"Please? Bailey. *Please.*"

There were actual tears in her eyes and I don't think she was forcing them.

And there it was. The death blow. The one I could never recover from. The weapon of mass emotional destruction.

"...Fine," I whispered.

And... my intestines have been replaced by snakes. Writhing, squirming, hissing and probably poisonous snakes.

Why am I like this?

"I KNEW you'd say yes!" She squealed and threw her arms around me, engulfing me in a cloud of perfume and my impending doom. "Ahhhhh, I'm so excited! Thank you, thank you, thank you!"

Before I could tell her she was welcome—or fake my own death—Knox returned.

He walked toward us with a tray stacked with bagels and a variety of cream cheeses like the world wasn't seconds away from ending.

"Hey," he said. "More bagels for the table. I brought cinnamon raisin, everything, and strawberry sourdough. There's plain cream cheese, honey pecan, and one that might be strawberry but also might be pink glue."

"Just in time!" Jessa said, and her fingertips were digging into my wrist again. "Bailey, tell him the good news!"

Knox glimpsed at me, then Jessa, then back again.

"Bailey!" Jessa jostled me. "Tell himmmmmmmm."

"Um. We're going to be in the kissing contest." I whispered, with a full-body wince I hope Jessa didn't notice.

Knox almost dropped the tray. A strawberry sourdough bagel fell to the ground, landing on its side, and rolled away like a rogue tire.

What I wouldn't give to just... stop, drop, and roll away... like that.

"I'm sorry—what?" Knox asked.

I fanned myself. Was it just me or was it suddenly very hot out?

"You two are *Couple Number 25*. I asked for 11, because that's my lucky number, but..." She shrugged and shook it off. "It doesn't matter. This is gonna be *iconic*."

She stood up. Grabbed my shoulders.

"I love you," she said, then she turned and pointed at Knox. "And I love you!"

She kissed him on one cheek, then the other.

He looked at me. I looked at him.

"Wait," he said. "No. No. We're not... kissing. We're not..."

There was something in his eyes. Not just frustration. Not just surprise. A flicker of something else I couldn't put a name to. But it was gone so fast, I couldn't be sure I hadn't imagined it.

"You're in. Bailey already said yes on your behalf," Jessa informed him.

"Bailey said yes on my behalf," Knox echoed, in a tone I'd never heard him use. Somewhere between mad and hollow.

"Of course she did. I can always count on your girl,

Knoxxy. She's always such a team player!" Jessa clapped her hands together.

"It's why we love her," Greer chimed in.

Jessa sashayed off, humming a wedding march remix and probably planning our future children's names, which might be timely since it felt like a bowling ball was gestating in my gut.

Knox set the tray down on the table, very slowly. "You said yes on my behalf?"

"I... didn't... I didn't want to."

"But you did."

"I can't disappoint people!"

His brow furrowed. "Well. We'll beg to differ about that."

My mouth dropped open.

"You... Did you just... Are you saying I disappointed you?" I asked, eyebrows raised. Heat rushed up my back, my neck, spreading to my ears and cheeks.

"Bailey, we both agreed that it would be very, very bad if word got out in Serenade Creek that we were romantically involved. The town tour, remember? How cautious we were not to let anyone see us holding hands? Now you want to kiss in front of the entire town?"

I hadn't thought about that. In the moment, I could only think about not letting Jessa down.

"Well, I doubt the entire town will be there, but no, I don't want to kiss you in front of whoever will be there!"

He shook his head. Raked his hand through his hair. "I just told you I can't date you, Bailey," he said, his voice low, soft. "And the first thing you do is sign us up for a kissing contest?"

I closed my eyes for a second, because I wasn't going to

shed a tear. Not now. When he was standing there, all but accusing me of trying to manipulate him into dating me?

"Okay, I did not sign us up for a kissing contest," I said, my voice sharp. "I agreed when *your* friend begged me to because I don't want to ruin her wedding." I stood up. "You could've told her no, and shut the whole thing down, and you didn't."

"Because you already said yes for both of us."

"Well, she wasn't asking me to kiss myself! I can't say no, Knox! I mean, I can, but it's really hard for me and I wish it wasn't but it is and you know that! She backed me into a corner and there were tears," I cried. "My goodness. I thought you understood me, but apparently you don't at all, so your inability to date me is doing us both a big favor."

"Where are you going, Bailey?" he asked as I started to walk away. "We need to make a plan—"

"I got us into it. I'll get us out of it," I cut him off. "We don't need to do anything because there is no *we*. And you don't have to worry! You were perfectly clear about that, Knox."

Then I marched off, hopefully in the same direction my dignity had wandered off to.

CHAPTER ELEVEN

KNOX

If you'd told me a few days ago I was going to get to kiss Bailey Cooper again, I would have told you, yeah, right, maybe in my dreams.

If you'd told me I was going to kiss Bailey Cooper again, but in front of the whole town of Serenade Creek, and be awarded points for my creativity or lack thereof, yeah, those dreams just took a hard left into the land of my worst nightmares, especially since the Hearts & Charts Brigade are the judges.

It might all be moot, because Bailey's missing.

She and the other bridesmaids had gone to Wisteria Bridal Co. this afternoon for some last-minute alterations and fittings. Everyone else had come back as a group, but according to Greer, Bailey said she needed to swing by her place for some vague purpose and insisted they leave without her. We were all trying to keep it from Jessa so she wouldn't spiral over someone 'leaving the bubble'.

The Serenade Creek Amphitheater was packed. Not with casual looky-loos who just want to see what's up and then mosey on to the next attraction, but with *we brought coolers and snacks and folding fans shaped like hearts and we are here for the duration* diehard fans planning to stay for all the extra innings. These people were way too excited about watching other people kiss.

The stage itself was decorated with crepe paper streamers, pink balloons, and a massive sign that says *PUCKER UP, SERENADE CREEK!* in letters so sparkly I thought glitter may have just gone on the endangered species list.

"Knox! Knoxathon!" Iris, seated between Cornelia and Ruby at the judge's table, was flagging me down with one end of Ruby's ubiquitous scarf. "Yoo-hoo! Knoxander!"

There was a woman on stage I didn't recognize with a microphone and a clipboard strutting and cheesing and hamming it up like she was hosting the thirtieth season of *America's Got Tongue* on prime-time television. Why were there so many clipboards in this town and why were the women of Serenade Creek dead set on weaponizing them?

"And remember, folks, this year's kissing contest is going to be judged in three categories: chemistry, creativity, and crowd reaction! So don't be afraid to give us a little sizzle!"

Jessa had been texting me *Chemistry! Creativity! Crowd Reaction!* approximately every twenty minutes all day, so those were drilled into my brain, but I couldn't even think about sizzle.

"Knoxtopher!" Iris called, and that was followed up by a high-pitched whistle. I glanced over. Stanley was helping her out. I waved them both off and hurried to where my fellow groomsmen were standing off to the side of the hustle and bustle, trying to look like they were way too cool to be at such an event. Let's be honest: Almost everyone is too cool to be at this kind of event. Even Stanley.

I tugged at my collar which seemed to be getting tighter and tighter by the minute.

"Have any of you seen Bailey?" I whispered to them.

"What do you mean, have we seen Bailey?" Luke hissed, grabbing my arm and pulling me over to the side, away from the others. "You lost her? Did she pull a Runaway Bride?"

"I think to pull a Runaway Bride, she has to *be* a bride."

"But she's not here?" He blinked, shook his head, blinked again and made a face like he was standing downwind from a skunk's fart. I glanced to our left and there was Corey, so, yeah, the skunk's fart thing tracks. Love him like a brother, but he's a gassy dude. "Bro," Luke said, and he was shaking his head again, but his disgust was definitely aimed at me. "What the actual what are you wearing?"

He and Jessa had gotten here later than the rest of us, since they had to deal with a catering crisis, so he hadn't seen me in the getup his dearly beloved decided I should wear this evening.

I looked down at myself and kind of recoiled too. I think my brain kept trying to come down with a case of temporary amnesia when it came to my attire: a suit that, I guess, was cream-colored underneath all the endless overlapping heart patches in seventy-five or so different shades of pink, red, and purple that had apparently been sewn on with glittering gold thread. Underneath: pink shirt. Red bowtie. On my head: Ridiculous matching top hat.

"Is it that bad?" I asked, deadpan.

Luke burst out laughing. I wiped at the corner of my eye, where I think a drop of his spittle landed, and was getting ready to fester into an awesome case of conjunctivitis. Which would at least match with this outfit.

"Jessa wanted Bailey and I to match," I said. "She thought it would give us a leg up, make us stand out, etc."

"Well, it will definitely make you stand out," he grimaced. Then he laughed. "You look so ridiculous. Like the mascot off a box of cereal. Love-Os. The breakfast that gives you a little sugar." He made a kissy-face at me.

I stared at him, my face solemn, like I was mad. Then I clapped him on the back and grinned, "You're marrying my stylist, bro. Enjoy your new wardrobe. Now, if you happen to see a pretty lady in a dress made of this lovely fabric, let me know, alright?"

"Wait, for real though. You don't know where Bailey is?"

"I'm sure she's..."

I sighed. When it came to Bailey, I wasn't sure about anything.

She hadn't spoken to me since she'd stormed off at brunch, unless you count a note that said: *Jessa did the robot short-circuiting thing again. We're not getting out of it. I'm sorry.*

It was now 6:30 p.m. The kissing contest began at seven.

"Find your girl," Luke said. "And please don't let mine know you lost her."

"She's not..." I bit my lip. "How upset do you think Jessa would be if Bailey and I got in a fight, broke up, and Bailey bailed?"

Because that's the story we might have to go with. My palms were sweaty, so I didn't think it was that farfetched to imagine her getting spooked and making a run for it once she saw the crowd.

Or maybe yet another person had harassed her about the

whole Eternal Bouquet curse and it had finally been too much and she was alone somewhere, tears in those beautiful eyes...

Or maybe my reaction—my unreasonably harsh reaction—at brunch had been what was too much for her.

That was what I was the most concerned about.

And I owed her an apology.

Luke blinked at me some more. "You guys can't break up because you aren't really together and if she bailed, I want my money back. Every dime."

He shook his head.

He wasn't upset about the money and we both knew it.

"Do you think she bailed? Jessa will flip. She'll..." his voice trailed off.

I sighed. Shoved my hands in my pockets. "I don't know, man. I was a little... I think I hurt Bailey's feelings."

"You don't hurt people's feelings. You're the nicest guy I know."

"I just—"

"Contestants," the emcee was yapping again. "You need three things! You need your number. It must be attached to your chest at all times. You need your partner, obviously. And you need some lip balm, because if you're doing this right, you're gonna need some aftercare. Oh, and everybody suck a breath mint and get ready! We're starting the count-down clock."

"Hey," Luke said.

"What?"

"Do you really have feelings for Bailey?"

"No," I said. "You know I'm not going down that road again—"

He shook his head. "I can't believe it. You do. You're really into her."

"I...I gotta go," I said.

I craned my neck, looking around one more time.

My heartbeat quickened as I spotted her.

She was wearing the same long cotton candy pink wig from last summer. The same oversized heart-shaped sunglasses. And, of course, the dress that matched my suit, but she didn't look ridiculous at all.

I bobbed and weaved through the other contestants—a lot of flashy people in Serenade Creek, apparently—and got to her before she could slip out of sight again.

"Hey," I said. "You okay?"

"Hey," she said. "I'm sorry about this morning. I—"

I shook my head. "Don't apologize. I'm the one who should be doing that. Bailey, I—"

"I thought I could wear this disguise and maybe, you know, give them a fake name to announce so not everyone would know it was me you were kissing, but yeah, the Hearts & Charts Brigade had already seen the sign-up sheets, so..." She took a deep breath and let it out and I really wanted to hug her in that moment more than I wanted to kiss her. "But I came up with another plan. I told Jessa that you and I have to be discreet, you know, because of school district policy, so if we're going to do this we have to pretend we're not actually dating, but doing it for a good cause and—"

"Shhh," I said. "Slow down. It's okay."

"It's not okay. The countdown has started. I need a paper bag to breathe into," she let out a few exaggerated exhales. "Knox, I caught the bouquet again. The Eternal Bouquet....I don't think anyone knows about it yet—except the other bridesmaids and Mabel—but...," she looked around, her brow furrowed. "I'm six times cursed now. I need to keep a low profile. Winning a kissing contest because you and I sizzled is the last thing I need right now. Can we like, just do a quick peck and tell Jessa—"

"Yeah," I said. "I'll tell her... I got stage fright and froze. I'll take the heat. Don't worry about it. Just a quick peck. Close your eyes and think of England."

I cringed. Did I actually just say that?

But she laughed, and the sound... I don't not love the sound of her laughter. She always sounds caught off guard to be laughing, but in the best way, like she hadn't expected it, but it was a pleasant surprise.

"No one is going to believe you have stage fright, though. You perform... voluntarily... in front of kids on a regular basis —shockingly honest kids. Kids who will laugh at you and call you a dork to your face."

I feigned offense. "You think I'm a dork?"

She tilted her head, as if genuinely considering it. "Well. You do have a label maker."

"That is not dorky. That is prepared."

"It is dorky *and* prepared," she said.

"I'm going to take that as a compliment."

"You probably alphabetize your spices, don't you?"

"Doesn't everyone?"

Our banter had been like this during that week last summer. Easy. Teasing. And it ended with us kissing every time.

I cleared my throat. "Um, how did you catch the Eternal Bouquet again? Did you sneak off to a wedding?"

She shook her head. "No, I... it is truly unbelievable. Mabel keeps it at Wisteria Bridal Co.—where the others were getting last minute alterations on their dresses and I was having my fitting. It stays on this pedestal on a little round stage. Under an actual spotlight. Well, anyway, Melody's dress was too long and she tripped and knocked over the pedestal and the Eternal Bouquet was falling and I was standing right there and Mabel cried *Catch it, Bailey!* and so... I did, not even thinking, you know, that I was *catching the bouquet* until I was holding it again. You can laugh."

"I'd never laugh at you, Bailey," I smiled at her. "With you, yeah, but... at you? Never."

I opened my mouth to say something else—something calm, something reassuring—but before I could, she asked, "Hey, are you okay?"

"Yeah, I—"

"Couples one through ten, final call! If your number is pinned to your chest and your lips are ready for action, now's the time to step up! Don't make me send the Hearts & Charts Brigade down there to collect you!"

Bailey groaned softly. "They would absolutely do that, too. With a big old human-sized butterfly net."

"We're couple twenty-six," I said. "We've got a little time before they call us. Come on. Let's just... blend."

We walked over to a low stone wall on the edge of the amphitheater.

"Your mouth as dry as mine?" she asked.

"Mm-hmm. I'll go get us a couple bottles of water."

When I returned, we sat in silence, shoulder to shoulder, watching the chaos of couples one through ten play out onstage. It felt... easy. Familiar. Like this was the most normal thing in the world: sitting next to Bailey Cooper. The only thing that felt wrong was pretending not to feel everything I wasn't supposed to feel.

Then.

I offered her my hand. Without thinking. Without meaning to. Without immediate regret, though I'd have the guilt later.

She hesitated for half a second—probably debating whether or not this touching was unnecessary and hence against her rules—then grabbed it, pressing her palm against mine, folding her fingers down between mine, like they'd always belonged there.

"Knox," she whispered, eyes still wide behind those giant sunglasses, "if I pass out up there, you're legally obligated to drag me offstage by the ankles."

"When we're up there, if you feel light-headed or faint, why don't you just grab onto my shoulders, just as a precautionary measure? I'll make sure you don't hit the floor."

She hesitated again. "I didn't agree to this to trick you into... anything."

"I know you didn't."

"Okay. Well. If I feel light-headed or faint, I will grab your shoulders in a totally platonic way."

"Or we can call this whole thing off, if you want?" I offered. "We can make a run for it."

"I don't know if running for it is an option. I think I've lost all feeling in my legs."

"Are you that nervous or did you go too hard during the wheelbarrow race?"

"Combination, I think."

A collective gasp went up as Couple Number 14 broke apart onstage, and the guy dipped his unsuspecting partner— almost dropping her.

"Do not dip me," Bailey said, clutching my hand tighter.

"I won't," I said.

"Just a peck."

"Just a peck."

"Jessa's gonna kill us."

"Well, we'll have a few days to live. She doesn't have time to get wheelbarrows for Greer and Corey to push our corpses down the aisle in, so we're safe 'til after the wedding."

Bailey laughed again, then we fell into comfortable silence until our group was called up. We walked back to the stage so slowly that by the time we got there, Couple Number 24 was bowing to half-hearted applause.

Then we both turned our attention to Couple Number 25, who brought their own music to which they reenacted every dance number from Dirty Dancing in sixty seconds, including the lift, after which the guy seamlessly lowered the girl down to her tiptoes and they ended in a kiss that had us all blushing.

"We did not come prepared," Bailey said.

"Unh-unh, not at all."

"Thank you Sierra and Alex Pennington who unofficially just swept the creativity points category. Our next liplockers are both familiar faces to Serenade Creek, but they're not a couple, in the romantic sense. Bailey Cooper is the art teacher at Serenade Creek Elementary and Knox Showalter is the assistant principal. They're gracing our stage with their presence—and lips—to raise awareness for the Love to Learn Fund."

I looked at Bailey.

"Stupid?" she asked.

I shook my head. "Brilliant."

"I'm sorry I got us into this," she whispered as we climbed the steps.

My heartbeat was pounding in my chest—and not because I had stage fright.

"Oh, you're going to be sorry," I squeezed her hand. "I forgot my breath mint *and* my lip balm."

And apparently my mind, my common sense, and my conscience, because what was I doing? I was flirting with her. I hadn't intended to... but I had.

She removed my hat and placed it off to the side of the stairs.

Then she nodded at me.

We took our places center stage, facing each other.

Stanley shouted, "That's my boy!" while Ruby screamed some unintelligible and probably obscene encouragement. Iris apparently had gotten a chant going, "KNOXLEY, KNOXLEY, KNOXLEY!"

"Iris is determined to elongate my name," I whispered to Bailey, who'd gotten paler and paler.

She shook her head and replied, quietly, "No, I think that's actually our couple name. You know, a combination of Bailey and Knox."

So apparently the audience had not heard the part in our intro about not being a romantic couple. Or they'd just decided they'd collectively will it into being, maybe, with a combination of vocal synchronicity and Serenade Creek magic.

"Oh."

Her sunglasses had slipped down so I could see the panic in her eyes. I gently lifted them off her face and stuck them in my suit-coat pocket.

Then I ran my knuckles down the side of her face.

"Just a peck," I repeated, though something inside me was already unraveling.

"Just a peck," she echoed, barely audible.

I took a step towards her. She met me halfway.

And when our lips touched, lightly, barely—just a brush —I felt it as much as I felt our very first kiss. It seemed like a lifetime ago. It seemed like yesterday.

No explosions of fireworks. No choirs of angels singing. Just this quiet, aching rush

in my veins. A kind of stillness, like everything in the world had melted away except the place where her mouth met mine. Peace, with joy sparking at the edges.

It should have ended there.

Just a peck.

We could've pulled back.

Just a peck.

Smiled for the crowd.

Just a peck.

Left everyone believing we were just here to raise awareness for the fundraiser.

We should've pulled back. No, I should've pulled back.

But I didn't. And she didn't, either.

I kissed her.

I kissed her like she was mine. Like she always had been.

She let out the softest sound. A tiny gasp, like the wind had been knocked out of her.

And then she kissed me back.

Bailey leaned into me—pressed close—and her hand slid up to my chest, curling into my shirt like she needed something solid to hold on to.

Like she needed me.

And a still quiet voice, buried somewhere deep, whispered, *You need her too.*

Whatever self-control I'd barely been hanging onto snapped, quietly.

My blood roared. My heart pounded. Everything in me ached—not just with want, but with longing. That deep, painful kind of longing that leaves claw marks behind.

The crowd disappeared. The noise evaporated.

It was just me and Bailey and her soft, searching lips. Familiar and new all at once.

When we pulled apart, it happened slowly, like the world had gone still and time forgot how to tick.

Her eyes met mine.

My heart was out of control. I could hardly catch my breath.

There was silence. Then a murmur rippled through the crowd—soft gasps, a scattered "whoa," and then something else. Applause.

I didn't hear most of it, not really. But somewhere in the back of my mind, I registered the sound. And still—I couldn't look away from her.

"Oh, no," she whispered, jokingly. "I think we sizzled."

But her eyes weren't laughing. It wasn't just surprise in her gaze.

It was hope.

And I was the one who'd put it there.

Right in front of the whole town.

CHAPTER TWELVE

"Come here often?"

The voice—Knox's voice—broke through my thoughts and I looked up to see him standing far enough to say, 'I'm going to keep my distance if that's what you want' but close enough to say, 'I'm not opposed to joining you if you ask'.

I let out a slow breath and gave him a smile even though my mouth muscles protested.

"You didn't have to come looking for me," I told him.

He shook his head. "I, uh, didn't. I was looking for a quiet place to think."

"Well." Without feeling offended—I appreciated his honesty—I made a 'move along' gesture with my hand. "Keep looking. I have dibs here."

I was joking. Kind of?

Part of me wanted to say, "Hey, sit down with me. Let's talk."

Part of me recognized—and was resisting—the fact that I could easily morph into Lady Bailey of Longington: "Sir Knox, you must kiss me again or I'll perish! I will! The marrow in my bones is shriveling from lack of your touch."

"Yeah. I'll go. Of course. You were here first." He nodded, and turned to go, but then turned back. "This place isn't on the map of the grounds," he said, holding up the crumpled map like it was Exhibit A.

This place was a secluded, quiet spot where a path bordered by fringe trees opened up to reveal the swing I was sitting in. It hung from a thick wooden arch, with trellised walls, the whole structure woven through with fairy lights and climbing roses that looked like they'd been dipped in sunset. The ropes were thick, slightly frayed, weathered just enough to whisper that this place had been used, cherished— even if it wasn't on any map. The full moon was directly overhead, casting just enough light to make everything feel a little magical.

"The Enchanted Rose Inn has secrets," I said. "Or so they say. Places you only find when you need them."

"Huh. So... is it just a coincidence, you think, that we both found this particular place tonight?"

I shrugged. What should I say to that? What did he want me to say to that? Certainly not, "Oh, Sir Knox. Of course 'twas not coincidence, but fate that led you to me this moonlit eve."

Cherish would say it wasn't a coincidence. Cherish quite often said there were no coincidences in Serenade Creek.

"Do you really want me to leave, Bailey?" he asked, softly.

I nodded, because... I should. Then shook my head because... I didn't. Then patted the empty space beside me.

There was room enough for us to both sit without touching. "We should probably make a plan, for going forward. So... what happened today doesn't happen again."

"Oh, you think Jessa might try to trap you into another kissing contest, huh?"

I shook my imaginary Magic-8 ball and glanced down at it. "Signs point to yes."

He got the reference, and laughed. "Yeah. She is psyched about winning the spot in the hot air balloon parade—by the way, I'm afraid of heights, so... that's gonna be fun—and henceforth, is likely to enter us in any contest in which we might score her a prize."

"Henceforth," I mocked, lightly.

Yeah. We won the kissing contest.

By a landslide.

With a perfect score.

The only perfect score.

After the kiss, there'd been a beat of silence.

Then... cheering.

The kind of cheering that wasn't just polite.

The kind of cheering people saved for last-minute buzzer beaters when the underdog wins.

We didn't talk as we walked offstage.

We barely looked at each other.

I'd been afraid of what might fall out if I opened my mouth.

And even now, I pressed my lips together until it hurt, in case they might accidentally auto-pucker.

I stopped pushing against the ground with my toe, to let the swing come to a stop, so he could sit down. Once he was settled, he took over gently swaying us to and fro. Who says to and fro? A woman who has had a sizzling kiss with the guy she wants but cannot have in front of the whole town, whose brain is slowly shutting down as a result. That's who.

"How many texts have you gotten?" I asked him.

Before we could even get back to the inn, I'd had eighty-seven—and I'm not even counting the ones from my friends.

You two are ADORABLE.

That chemistry?? Bailey Cooper. Girl. I didn't know you had it in you.

The Eternal Bouquet always works. Better late than never.

Y'all officially are on the spreadsheet! THANK YOU, BAILEY! XOXO The Cupids

"Too many to count," he paused.

"I'm sorry," I said.

"It's not your fault," he said.

"Well..." I said.

"Did you get a lot of voicemails, too?"

I scrunched up my nose. "Who leaves voicemails?"

"The school board president's assistant, apparently," he said.

That made me blink. "What? Are we in trouble?"

"Oh, to the contrary. He called to say how much they're looking forward to seeing me—and my *lovely girlfriend*—at the donor breakfast in August."

I winced.

"I messed up."

I said it.

But he also said it.

At the exact same time.

Neither of us said *jinx*, maybe because we were adults, maybe because we simply knew better.

"I let myself get caught up in it," he said. "I shouldn't

have. I told myself I would not give you mixed signals... and I keep giving you mixed signals... and I'm sorry."

"You don't have to explain," I said softly. "You already said it can't happen. We can't date. I heard you loud and clear. I really didn't say yes to the kissing contest to try to trick you or trap you into anything. I just... I was trying to make Jessa happy."

"Bailey, I know," he said. "You've already told me and even if you hadn't, it never even crossed my mind that you could have a manipulative bone in your body. You are a lot of things, but you're not nefarious."

A lot of things, huh? Tell me more, sir.

Oh, stop that.

We can't date. We can't date. We can't date.

But that kiss...

I inhaled, breathing in the soapy-sweet night air, wishing I could bottle the scent. Hating that it would now always remind me of this night.

"The fringe trees," I said as I pointed at them, at their branches laden with the shimmery, creamy white fringe-like petals they were named for. "They should've stopped blooming in May but inexplicably still seem to be at their peak."

"Serenade Creek magic?"

"Maybe."

We fell silent for a moment, both looking at the trees.

And then, almost too soft to hear: "I used to think love was the whole point."

My breath caught.

I turned to look at him, though he remained facing forward, his hands clasped in his lap.

"That with the right person, not only could you survive

anything, but that happily ever after was a foregone conclusion. I believed, whole-heartedly believed. In... all of it. The grand gestures. The promises. The forever."

I waited.

If he wanted to tell me, he would.

"My ex," he said, finally. "She wasn't just my first love. She was... everything. The girl next door. My best friend since I was five. High school sweetheart. We grew up together. Everyone thought we'd get married. And we almost did." He laughed, but with an edge of bitterness and zero humor. "For all intents and purposes, she left me at the altar."

The weight of it dropped between us like gravity.

The trees shivered around us.

He paused.

He still wasn't looking at me. His voice was steady, but I could hear the pressure building underneath it.

"Ten minutes before the ceremony, she told me she didn't think she'd ever really loved me, *not like that*." The way he said it. The way the words had the sharpness of a sword. Those were the exact words she'd used. "I can normally read people well. I see signs before anyone else does. I pick up on things, sometimes to my own detriment. But... I was blindsided."

I drew in a breath. Dug my fingers into my knees.

"I didn't believe her," he said, still staring straight ahead. "Not at first. I thought she was scared. Or overwhelmed. Or confused. But she wasn't."

"Oh, Knox," I said.

He finally turned to me. "She just didn't love me. And she waited until the very last second to tell me. The one person I thought I knew better than anyone else was the one person who had me thoroughly fooled."

I didn't breathe. Didn't blink.

Jessa's words came back to me:

You did the impossible, girlie. I didn't think he'd ever find love again. You must be something really special.

"My friends... my family... all of them think I just... closed off my heart. Put up walls. Gave up, shut down, refused to let anyone in."

"And you didn't?" I asked. "Sorry. Go on."

He looked at me now. Really looked at me. "This isn't a lecture, I promise, but don't apologize when you've done nothing wrong, okay? This is a conversation, not a soliloquy. You can ask questions."

"Okay," I said, softly.

"So, it all went down ten years ago. I tried for... several years. Tried to date. Tried to feel normal. Actually had a couple of very short-lived relationships."

I waited. Not because I didn't feel like I had any questions to ask, but... maybe because I had so many I couldn't choose which to ask first. Maybe because these answers were worse than if he'd just said, *I don't want you, Bailey.*

"It's not that I don't want to fall in love again. I wanted that very much at first. But... I don't think I can. I tried. I disappointed a few really great women." He sighed. "I think that part of me was broken, by her, and there's just not any fixing it."

He rubbed the back of his neck like he was trying to massage the memory away.

I waited.

"I think being unable to love is almost worse than being

unlovable," he said. "No one wants to be ruined, you know? But... I'm afraid I am."

I wanted to touch him. I wanted to wrap my arms around the broken part and tell him he wasn't alone, that I wasn't going anywhere.

But that would be too much.

"I'm sorry, Bailey."

"Hey," I said, gently, instead. "Don't apologize when you haven't done anything wrong."

He bumped his shoulder against mine and gave me a smile, though it seemed like his mouth might be protesting a bit, too.

A moment passed. Then two.

"Do you want me to give you your spot back?" he asked. "Or we can go down to the firepit? All the others are still there. Or we can go back to the room?"

"Yeah," I said, standing. "I am kind of tired. You can go hang with your friends if you want, but I think I'll turn in."

He stood, too. "No, I'll walk back with you. If that's okay."

I sighed, but I didn't realize I'd done it until a shadow crossed his face. A flicker of something in his eyes.

"Oh. Is it not okay?"

"No, no," I touched his hand. Oops. Didn't mean to do that either.

Bailey Cooper, could you just, like, not lose complete control of yourself?

"It's not that I don't want you to come along. It's just that I was planning to wander. Meander. You know. Take the long way back."

He chuckled. "Well, since I actually have no idea which

way even is back, wandering and meandering was definitely on my agenda."

We got up and set off down the winding path, walking side by side, mostly quiet. Then I began oohing and ahhing over every statue, every water feature, every nighttime bloom that looked like it had been touched by magic, though, let's be honest, most likely none of them had.

"I want to see every inch of this place. I've lived in Serenade Creek all my life," I told him. "And this is my first time at the Enchanted Rose Inn. When my friends and I were little, at sleepovers, we would pretend we were staying here instead of one of our houses and would take turns getting to be the bride who was getting married here." I covered my cheeks with my hands. "I can't believe I just told you that. How embarrassing."

"Nah, it's sweet. Did you use pillowcases as veils?"

I burst out laughing. "We did. My friend Kelsie had an older sister and she had this satin white robe and we always stole it to use as the wedding gown."

"And let me guess... when you took turns, you were always last? Always like, no, Kelsie, you go next. Get ya man, girl. I can wait."

I side glanced at him. His eyebrows were raised. There was zero judgement. Just curiosity and a little something else I couldn't put a label on and didn't want to. Seeing me. That's what it was. He was seeing me. Maybe even accepting me?

He was emotionally unavailable. That's all I needed to know.

"Old habits die hard," I shrugged. "But I assure you, I never, as a nine-year-old, said *get ya man*."

He chuckled and I smiled despite myself. He had a really great laugh.

"Well," he said. "If nothing else, I'm glad you finally got to stay here. I wish it could've been under better circumstances."

Remembering we were supposed to make a plan, I said, "Well, maybe we can make our circumstances better."

His brows were up again. "How so? Because if your idea is to get a replacement Knox to be your fake boyfriend, unfortunately, I think Jessa would probably notice."

I smiled. "She might. But, no, I..." I took a deep breath and why does this place have to even *smell* like love? I exhaled, then said, "We're here. We have to pretend to be a couple. Let's just... have fun with it. Like we did last year at the Summer Lovin' Festival. No expectations. After it's over, we just go back to the way we were. But... let's enjoy ourselves. Maybe if we're actually having a good time, that'll take some of the pressure off pretending. We'll at least look happy without having to force it, right?"

He pressed his lips together and looked up at the sky, as if he was deep in thought. Then he grinned at me. "I hate weddings. No. I dread weddings. I've been dreading this wedding, as much as I'm happy for Luke and Jess. This next few days are not going to be easy for me, so... I actually love that idea, Bailey Cooper. Fun, huh?"

It was hard to think of Knox as dreading anything, but I'm glad he told me. "I mean... I think we can."

"Well... tomorrow is the scavenger hunt and scavenger hunts and fun are pretty synonymous, so... is there a better time to try? Hey," he said, abruptly. "Bailey, look."

I followed the direction he was pointing and didn't see anything... at first. Then I gasped at the pinprick of light. A firefly. Though they'd been promised, we hadn't seen any while camping. Like hearts, nature does what it wants, I suppose.

We watched for a few minutes and the longer we stood still, the more appeared, winking in and out, like dancing stars come to earth.

"Wow," he said.

Finally, we started walking again, and fell into a light and easy back-and-forth conversation and too soon, we were back inside the grand entrance of the inn.

Knox followed me up the stairs. I unlocked the door and pushed it open and gasped.

"What is it?" he asked from behind me.

"I think we've been robbed." I stepped out of the way so he could see into our suite.

"Jessa is officially out of control," he said, shaking his head.

"Uh, Jessa has been officially out of control for some time, but... she took the couch."

"Well," he said, walking over to the empty spot on the rug where it used to be, as if it had just gone invisible and bumping into it might solve the mystery. "Maybe she didn't take it? There are renovations going on, right? Maybe they're just reupholstering the couches?"

I walked over to the bed and picked up the small box and piece of monogrammed stationery. "Well, let's see. There's a box of Breathe Better nasal strips and a note. *Snuggle up, buttercups! Just helping the cutest couple in Serenade Creek keep the love alive! THAT KISS, THOUGH!!! Jessa.*"

I looked at Knox.

"She is truly diabolical," he shook his head. "I can sleep

on the floor. Supposedly, it's good for your back. Or maybe on the window seat?"

"Because you're secretly a contortionist? Might as well sleep in the bathtub," I said.

"I don't think it'd be that bad," he said but his face was far less certain than his words.

"Listen," I said, trying to sound way more relaxed than I felt. "This is silly. It's a king-sized bed. We're adults. We'll stay on our own sides and pretend the Grand Canyon's between us. It's not like either of us has cooties." I arched my brow. "Unless...maybe you do?"

"Well, if I did, you probably already caught them back at the kissing contest, so—"

"Oh, no," I said as something else caught my eye. "Oh, no, no, no, no."

"Okay, yeah. I get it. I made things worse by bringing up the kissing contest and now you're uncomfortable. We can figure something else out—"

"Knox, no. Look." I pointed at the vase.

"Oh, the Furniture Fairy snatched our couch and left a flower in exchange. Classy."

"No, Knox. That's not a flower. That's an Enchanted Rose."

He looked confused. Of course he did. He didn't spend his childhood trading Enchanted Rose Inn lore with his friends instead of spooky urban legends or ghost stories.

I walked over to it and by the vase, there was another piece of Jessa's stationery.

Without touching it, I leaned down and read her neat script.

Bailey! All the girls are wearing these in their hair tomorrow! Don't forget it!

"Oh, no," I moaned. "We're doomed. DOOMED."

I turned around to face him. "That," I pointed at the most exquisite rose I'd ever seen in my life, "is an Enchanted Rose. It's the rose the inn was named after because they only grow here."

"Okay, so rare rose. Why does it doom us?"

"Well. It's not actually enchanted, obviously. Except maybe it is? Legend has it that when someone lies in its presence, it wilts."

"So it... is enchanted."

"No. I mean. I don't know. But I guess we'll find out because according to Jessa, all the girls are wearing them in their hair tomorrow, and if I show up with a wilted rose in my hair..."

"We're doomed," he said.

I heaved a sigh.

"I just have one question."

He sounded so serious. "What is it?"

"Are we having fun yet?"

I'd paced back over to the bed while we talked and now, I picked up a pillow and hurled it at him. He caught it without hesitation.

"Yeah, you're totally sleeping in the bathtub, Mr. Comedian," I told him.

"Oh, Bailey Cooper. I think we'll both be far too worried about a rose exposing us as liars tomorrow to sleep at all."

CHAPTER THIRTEEN

KNOX

"Ooooooh," Jessa crooned, sweeping through the group of us like the love child of Cupid and a mad scientist.

She stopped between me and Bailey, putting her arms around us and pulling us in close. Tipping her head against Bailey's and then against mine, she whispered, sounding far more giddy than any human ever should be before 8:00 a.m., "Did you lovebirds have a good night's sleep?"

I leaned forward, meeting Bailey's gaze.

"Oh, did we ever. Right, hon?"

She stuck her tongue out at me before saying, "Soooo much cuddling. It was awesome."

Yes, awesome.

My favorite part was, hands-down, when I—determined *not* to touch Bailey—got so close to the edge of the bed that I rolled off and the thud of my body hitting the floor startled her awake. She had been so close to the edge—determined not to touch me—that she, too, fell off the bed and immediately joined me on the floor. The (fake) couple that crash-lands together stays together. Someone put that on a greeting card.

"Are you two ready to crush our Couples' Scavenger Hunt?" she asked, releasing us from her iron-clad grip.

"Has anyone ever told you you're a bit over the top?" I asked.

"Don't pretend that's not your favorite thing about me, Knoxxy," she said, pinching my cheek like she was my elderly aunt—who had been doing finger exercises.

"Serious question. You do know most of your brides-maids and groomsmen aren't couples, right? Yet most of the activities you've designed are for—"

"Mind your business." She narrowed her eyes but grinned as she flounced to the podium, where Luke was waiting. I couldn't help but smile, seeing the way he looked at her. The way she looked back.

Bailey was rubbing her shoulder. "What was that about?"

"Well, it's about our conniving bride and this whole week being a masterclass in invasive, unsolicited matchmak-ing." She probably did intensive online compatibility testing to make sure her pairings were on point.

Bailey let out an adorable little gasp, her eyes going wide. "That's diabolical!" She grabbed my forearm and gave it a squeeze. "That's genius. That is... working. I think Greer and Corey were making eyes at each other last night. I thought it was just a trick of the candlelight, but... but hey!" She smacked my bicep lightly. "No unnecessary talking, remember?"

Bailey was insistent that Serenade Creek's love magic

was just silly superstitions. Maybe a little too insistent. Nonetheless, she said it was probably best if we didn't speak any more than what was strictly necessary while in Jessa's presence, as long as Bailey was wearing the Enchanted Rose in her hair.

We're telling enough lies on purpose. The less accidental lies we tell, the less this thing wilts, the lower our chance of being exposed as the fraudsters we are, she'd said.

I peeked at the rose, which she'd tucked behind her ear, securing it with an army of bobby pins.

Catching me checking, Bailey asked, "Is it okay?"

I nodded. Obviously I didn't believe in a rose that could detect a lie and wilt in its presence, but better safe than sorry, right?

"Okay!"

Everyone, Bay and I included, snapped to attention at Jessa's voice.

"Oh, man, who gave her a microphone?"

"Like she wasn't loud enough, am I right?"

"I'm going to pretend I didn't hear you guys," Jessa said. "Which I can do, since none of you have mikes. Okay! I was going to give you all—except for Bailey and Knox, obviously —different partners today, but then I decided, if it's not broke, why fix it? I mean, you all are just so... compatible. It's uncanny."

I shot Bailey a knowing look.

"So... Luke is going to pass out disposable cameras..." her voice trailed off and she looked at Luke.

I exchanged glances with Bailey. There were no cameras, disposable or otherwise, in sight.

"Where are the cameras, hon?"

"Well, sweetums," Luke said. "I didn't want to upset you, but the delivery is a little behind."

"How behind?"

"They'll be here tomorrow. In plenty of time for the ceremony!"

"But we need them today, for the—"

"We can use our phones!" Bailey piped up, holding hers aloft.

Luke mouthed thank you at her, looking visibly relieved. Jessa relaxed, too. "Right. Of course. Everyone use your phones! That will actually be better, because we were going to have to wait for the film to be developed before we could announce the winners."

I smiled at Bailey.

"Luke is going to give you maps of the property where all of the stations are marked. You do not have to do them in order! This scavenger hunt isn't about finding items, ladies and lads. It's about collecting moments. It's about speed. It's about accuracy. It's about looooooooooooooove. The first couple back here with their completed list will be declared the winners. Pics or it didn't happen, folks!"

"What do we win?" Sasha asked.

"Winning is the win, Sash," Rafe shook his head—disappointed—as if she should know this already.

"The winning couple gets a couples massage and sauna, makeovers, and a romantic dinner—your favorite dishes, specially curated by our caterer—for two under the stars!"

"Wait, like a romantic dinner and couples massage with..." Greer pointed back and forth between herself and Corey. "With each other?"

"She loooooooooves him," Bailey whispered.

Luke handed me our map.

"On your marks," Jessa said.

"We throw this, right?" Bailey whispered, after Luke was out of earshot, moving on to Melody and Blain.

"Oh, we throw it hard," I agreed, then added, "I mean, makeovers? Like the two of us could get any better-looking?"

She snorted and... yeah, I found it attractive.

"Get ready! And..." Jessa paused, dramatically. "Go!"

No one moved except for Rafe and Sasha and I think he was dragging her. I guess Bay and I weren't the only ones who had decided to throw it.

"I said go!" Jessa repeated.

"Can I have steak and lobster for dinner if we win?" Michael asked.

"You can have anything—and everything—you want! The sky's the limit!"

"And like, when you say makeovers?" Faye asked.

"The girls are low-key terrified Jessa's somehow going to manipulate it so we all have matching lobs for the ceremony," Bailey whispered.

"A lob? Like..." I mimicked throwing a ball in a high curve.

"I don't know what you're doing there, bud, but no," Bailey said.

I missed what Jessa had said, but all of a sudden, everyone was running.

My eyes widened as Bailey dropped to the ground. "Faye tripped me! Interference!"

I covered my mouth with my fist and faked a cough to suppress a laugh. Faye hadn't been within three feet of her, so unless she tripped Bailey with her telepathic powers...

"Oh, my gosh!" Jessa cried, rushing over. "Are you okay,

Bailey? Y'all! No playing dirty! I probably shouldn't have thrown in the cash prize."

She started to kneel down next to Bailey but I stepped in between them. "I've got her, Jess," I said. "Can you get up, baby?"

I hadn't called anyone baby in years, but it came out far too naturally.

And when I said it, Bailey's eyes met mine. For a split second. Then she turned her head, looking away.

Oh, right. No pet names was one of our rules... but hadn't those kind of gone out the window?

Something tightened in my chest.

"Yeah," Bailey said. "I'm not hurt. I can still do the competition. I want to win! I have WINERGY!"

"Yay!" Jessa clasped her hands together and bounced on her tiptoes.

"Yeah. Yay!" I said, but I was noticing the rose tucked behind Bailey's ear. The rose that hadn't wilted when she faked being tripped or when she enthusiastically proclaimed that she wanted to win—a lie, right?

I was still, for all intents and purposes, a newbie to Serenade Creek. What if there was some truth to the love magic? What if that Enchanted Rose did wilt upon hearing a lie?

Oh, my goodness. My dude. You are losing it.

Still.

It wasn't a chance I wanted to take.

As I helped Bailey up—and was it just my imagination or was her skin warmer each time I touched her?—I said to Jessa, as nonchalantly as possible, "You mentioned a cash prize. How much?"

"A grand."

Bailey's mouth dropped open. "As in a thousand dollars?"

Jessa grinned and nodded at Bailey. "Cash money, babes."

Bailey blinked.

She didn't look at me. Just stared at the map like it held all the answers. But even without eye contact, it was like I could read her mind: That was a few months of groceries and her car inspection and maybe, finally, that extra shelf of watercolor paper for her students who kept asking if they could take some home to practice.

"Okay," she said softly. "Okay."

"And the whole dinner under the stars thing? That's on the inn's property?" I asked.

"Of course, but I mean, y'all need to hustle if you wanna stand a chance," Jessa said. "Oh, and hey, our photographer sent assistants to film today and they're roaming all over so don't duck behind a topiary and do anything you wouldn't want preserved for posterity, huh?"

"We'll try to restrain ourselves," I promised.

Bailey had snagged our map from my loose grip and was examining it. "Station three is closest." She turned in a circle. "Thataway. I think."

"Lead the way," I said, and she began power walking. "Hey. Do you actually want to try to win this thing?"

She was a few paces ahead and glanced back at me, quizzically. "Why would I..."

"Bailey, stop for a sec," I called.

She did, turning to face me. "What is it?"

"Do you want to win this thing?"

"I—"

I shook my head. Closing the gap between us, I said, "Don't tell me what you think I want to hear right now. Don't think about what I want, or don't want."

"Knox..."

"I know what you teachers make. Not nearly enough. And almost everyone could use an extra grand, right?"

"But if we win the romantic dinner, Jessa isn't going to let us not have the romantic dinner—"

"Under the stars. On property. Tell me you don't want that. And before you do, please know that your eyes are literally lit up, just thinking about it, utterly betraying any people-pleasing you may be tempted to do right now."

Her eyes had lit up. And my pulse sped up.

It's just adrenaline, I told myself. The thrill of competition, I told myself.

Lies, lies, lies.

If her rose could read minds, it would've completely disintegrated.

She was hesitating.

"If we want to win, we need to go," I prompted, gently.

"Well... we said we'd have fun, right? And what's more fun than winning?"

"You don't have to justify it."

"Okay, okay!" she laughed. "Well then, I want to win."

"Yeah, you do," I said softly, and in that moment, I'm not sure I've wanted anything in a long time as much as I wanted to win this for her. I couldn't give her the kind of love she deserved. But I could give her this.

I held out my hand and she took it. Laced her fingers through mine.

And we took off running, the carefully curated landscape of the Enchanted Rose Inn's grounds blurring as we raced past.

"There are five envelopes left," Bailey said, plucking one from the basket, hanging from a shepherd's hook while I caught my breath. "We're the first at this station. Let's see..." She pulled out a card and read, "No love story's more romantic than that of Jack and Rose. Find the perfect location and strike a pose."

She looked up at me. "What is it?"

I'd been staring at her. I shook my head. Forced a smile. "Nothing. Just listening. Who are Jack and Rose?"

She shook her head and walked by me. "You did not just ask me that. Kate? Leo?" She glimpsed at me over her shoulder and I shrugged, helpless. "I'll explain during our romantic dinner under the stars. A gazebo will be perfect, and there's one... yes. This way. Come on, Knoxxy! Let's goooo."

I started to remind her that I hated being called that, but somehow, when Bailey said it, I actually didn't. Not at all.

"So I'm going to stand against the railing, with my arms like this." She swung them out wide. "Well, one arm out like that. I'll have to take the selfie with the other hand. Then you stand behind me, with your hands... erm, on my waist."

She seemed like she knew what she was doing, so I followed her instructions.

"Now smile pretty," she said.

Purdy purdy purdy, a cardinal echoed.

Bailey groaned as she took our picture.

"Okay, we got it. Now you're supposed to yell that you feel like the king of the world," she instructed.

"Wait... what?"

She laughed. "I'm joking. You've really never seen the Titanic?"

Dropping my hands, I stepped back to let her out from where she'd been pinned between me and the railing.

"I have not," I said. "The Titanic? Jessa couldn't find a happier love story for us to recreate? But don't they both die at the end?"

"I'll explain it over dinner. After we win. Let's go!" She grabbed my hand and we were running again and to be quite honest? I did sort of feel like the king of the world. Whatever that meant.

Greer and Corey were at the next station.

"I am NOT going to be known as Gorey," Greer said, her hands on her hips. "No way, no how."

"It's just a game," Corey said.

"Hey," Greer greeted us. "We're supposed to come up with our combined couple name, write it on the dry erase board, and take a picture. This tool wants us to be Gorey."

"And she thinks Coreer is better," Corey, obviously exasperated, said.

"Well, if you two aren't ready yet, mind it if we..." I pulled Bailey past them to the table.

I let her hand go, uncapped the marker, and wrote KNOXLEY.

"Oh, boo," Greer said, watching me. "You two are going to win all these competitions because you actually *like* each other."

"Are you saying you don't like me?" Corey dramatically put his hand over his heart. "I am mortally wounded."

I held up the sign and Bailey took the selfie.

"Let's go," I said.

"Good luck!" Bailey told them.

When we got to each of the next two stations, there were other non-coupled couples bickering and flailing. At one of the stations, we had to feed each other all of the wedding cake samples under a cloche. The other one was a trust walk in which Bailey took far too much satisfaction in blindfolding me. My trust in her was immediate, automatic, and made my stomach do a thing that had me wondering if I was having a reaction to all that frosting.

"We might actually have a chance," Bailey said as we walked past Melody and Blain who were sitting on a bench. He was wet and looked peeved. She was dry and looked pleased with herself.

"She let me trust walk right into the koi pond," he groused. "I got slapped by a lily pad."

I pressed my lips together. Then, as soon as we passed them, I said, "We so have a chance!" to Bailey.

"In your opinion, what is the most romantic spot on the Enchanted Rose property? Five minutes taken off your final time if you're..." Bailey's voice trailed off as she read the last clue.

"If you're what?"

She swallowed. "If you're smooching in the photo you take there. Jessa's word, not mine."

She scratched her forehead.

I consulted the map. "What about the Fountain of Forever? It's close and that sounds romantic?"

I'm almost certain she turned a shade lighter.

"You don't have any coins on you, do you?"

"No... why? Do we need to throw one in and make a wish or it's bad luck or something?"

She shook her head, quick. "No. No. We absolutely do not need to do that."

"Why is it called the Fountain of Forever?"

"No time for small talk! It's just another silly Serenade Creek legend," she said. "Let's run."

So we ran.

"Okay," she said when we got to the fountain. "Quick pic. Come on."

Offer. Do not offer. Offer. Do not—

"Wait... five minutes. Could be the difference between winning and losing... are you sure you don't want to...?" I raised my eyebrows in a way I hope was not lecherous.

She shook her head. Looked conflicted.

"Let me just..." She quickly pressed record on her phone, held it up and off to the side, and before I knew what was happening, she bounced up on her tiptoes and brushed her lips across mine.

Just a peck. Barely a kiss.

But it turned my heartbeat into a gong.

She fiddled with her phone. "Recording stopped. Just a little peckaroo, meant nothing, but totally counts, and I will FIGHT Jessa on that!"

As if her words had stirred the air itself, a gust of wind kicked up out of nowhere. Her hair whipped across her face, and with it—

The Enchanted Rose tumbled loose and to the ground.

The air went still again.

Not even a breeze.

I bent to retrieve the rose.

When I straightened, she was watching me with something unreadable in her eyes.

"That was... weird," she said, smoothing her hair back into place.

I stepped closer.

I reached out and tucked the rose behind her ear.

My fingers brushed her temple. Her skin. Her hair.

She smiled like it wasn't a big deal. Like it was nothing.

But... as inexplicably as what had happened with the wind, I felt something stir and kick up within me, and it felt a lot like a *But what if...*

CHAPTER FOURTEEN

BAILEY

"Okay," Knox said, later that afternoon, after the scavenger hunt—which we'd won by eighteen minutes—and lunch, when we were all gathered back at the Rose Garden Pavilion for the *mandatory but fun* (Jessa's words) dance practice. "I need you all to be gentle and non-judgmental with me. I know it's a big ask." He sent a pointed look in Jessa's direction. "But I am not a professional choreographer. I've never even taken a dance class."

I drew in a breath. I'd seen this man's moves and I found that awfully hard to believe.

Jessa grinned wickedly. "You sure about that, Knoxxy? Because I distinctly remember a certain talent show freshman year of college where a very cocky young man did a one-man rendition of *Bye Bye Bye* and you had to learn how to shake it somewhere..."

Greer chimed in, "He was Justin, JC, Lance, Joey, *and* Chris."

"Anyway," Knox said, ignoring them. "Our blushing bride asked me, as my wedding gift to her and Luke, to put together a little something we could all do together at the reception—"

Jessa cupped her hands around her mouth, "I didn't say little! After all, you know I'm over the top."

Butterflies were going wild in my stomach. I probably would've told Cherish *absolutely not* to take on this gig if I'd known I'd have to perform at the reception.

Huh. Somewhere along the way, I'd stopped thinking of it as a gig so doing so now threw me for a loop.

"So..." Knox clapped his hands together. "Can anybody Rumba?"

He looked at me.

I shook my head ever-so-slightly.

"Rumba? Like the robot vacuum?" Corey asked.

"I can't with you," Greer said, but the look in her eyes said she very much could with him, if only he'd ask her.

"Okay, no," Knox said, in the same patient voice he used with the students at school. "At the actual reception, Jessa and Luke will take the floor first, for their first dance. Then at regular intervals, the rest of us will filter in, one couple at a time, and join them—"

"Perfectly in sync!" Jessa sing-songed, but it kind of sounded like a threat.

"Perfectly in sync," Knox assured her. "Don't worry," he said to the rest of us. "I'll teach you what your cues will be and we'll practice a bunch. For now, just watch me and..."

He pointed at me and beckoned.

I shook my head again.

He nodded.

"Jessa, the music, please," he said, winking at me. Or

maybe he had something in his eye. Or was developing a twitch.

"Cue the music," Jessa said and a second later, the opening notes of SUV's "Weak" filtered in. Oh, great. Are we dancing to a slow '90s R&B jam or Bailey's Feelings: The Musical?

Knox walked towards me, reaching me at the exact moment the lyrics began. My knees indeed went weak and my heart fluttered like it had sprouted wings.

The way he looked at me caused me to ache in ways I didn't know was possible.

He bowed and held out his hand. "May I have this dance?"

"Can I say no?" I whispered, kind of joking. I'd slow danced at dozens and dozens of weddings, with everyone from my uncle to the mayor. I had no problem with slow dancing. I didn't even have a problem with slow dancing with Knox. I'd done it before. But I did experience full-body paralysis at the thought of slow dancing with Knox, with all of his friends watching. Somehow, it seemed more intimate than sharing a bed.

"Of course you can say no," he said. "I can get Jessa to—"

I shook my head.

If we were going to do this in front of everyone at the reception, I needed to practice.

Swallowing hard, I wrapped my fingers around his. And, of course: Goosebumps on my bare arms. Great. The body betrayal was unnecessary but real.

Holding his hand was getting way too easy and I already knew that once this week was over, I'd miss it.

For the first time this week, I wasn't afraid that Jessa or the others would see what I felt for Knox wasn't real. I was afraid he would see how it was becoming more real every time we touched, despite my common sense's constant red-flag waving.

I let him lead me to the center of the dance floor. Let me be honest: I'd probably let this man lead me over a cliff like a freaking lemur. Or was it a lemming? I was too far gone to remember.

He placed his hand on my waist, his touch light but sure, and adjusted our joined hands just slightly.

"You ready?"

I could barely nod. Because suddenly, his hand was on my back. Not in a possessive way. Not even inappropriate. Just... *there.* Warm. Firm. Anchoring.

"Just follow me," he said softly.

"Okay."

He stepped back, and I stepped forward. He turned, I turned. Slow, easy sway. Three steps, pivot. His hand skimmed from my back to my shoulder blade, steadying me. If Jessa had asked us to perform open-heart surgery as part of the wedding party duties, I'd have felt less out of my depth.

Knox spun me—nothing dramatic, just one of those slow, underhand turns that leaves your skin singing when his fingers glide along your arm. And then I was back in front of him.

"Let me guess," I said, breathlessly. "There's a dip coming up?"

I was joking. Trying to cut the tension with humor.

But he said, "You know it."

He turned me again, gentle and deliberate, and when I came back around, his hand slid up my spine, not in a flirta-tious way, but like... like he was memorizing the shape of something that would soon disappear. Or maybe I was just projecting.

It was pretend. All of this was pretend.

Except all the parts that weren't.

So many parts weren't.

My breath hitched when he dipped me just slightly, and my hand curled around the back of his neck on instinct.

He kept his eyes on me as we moved, every tiny step an invisible thread being pulled tighter between us.

"You can close your eyes if this close proximity eye contact is awkward with everyone watching."

"There are other people here?" I whispered, and that, too, was meant as a joke but it did not sound light-hearted. I jammed my eyes closed.

When I opened them again, his eyes were closed, but he was... be still, my heart... he was mouthing the lyrics. Like he wanted to sing along. Like he wanted to sing to me.

Oh, good grief, Bailey.

I hadn't been this swoony and ridiculous during my first slow dance, ever, with Byron Peebles, who I'd had a major crush on, in middle school.

Knox's eyes popped open.

Our mouths were... very close together, with only enough space for a tension that hummed and crackled, begging to be broken between us.

He can't fall in love! My common sense shrieked at me. *He can't! He told you he can't!*

But but but...

You asked him for the truth and he gave it to you! Believe it! Believe him.

But then...

He kissed me.

Not in a way that asked for permission.

Not in a way that tested the waters.

Not in a way that said, *Let's sell this, for Jessa's sake.*

He kissed me like a man who'd held back for too long, too hard, and the dam finally gave out.

Like he wanted to make sure *this* kiss lived in both our bones long after this week was over.

His hand slid up, cupping my cheek, his thumb trembling where it touched my skin. And it was that tremble that undid me. Because he wasn't unaffected. He wasn't controlled. He was coming undone, too.

It's not pretend, it's not pretend, it's not pretend.

I leaned into it, into him without thinking. Without breathing.

And when his other hand found the small of my back, when he pulled me closer like I was the one thing keeping him grounded to the earth, I *melted*. Right there. My knees, my will, my every defense—gone.

If this was pretend, it was the most honest lie I'd ever told.

If this was a mistake, it was the kind you regret with a smile, forever.

My fingers molded around his shoulders, gripping tight. Not to pull him closer, but to hold myself up. Because the floor wasn't steady anymore. Because the air around us felt too thin.

He kissed me like he was scared to stop.

And I kissed him back like I was scared to let him.

But when he finally did, his forehead dropped to mine. "Bailey," he whispered, like a confession. Like a prayer. Like my name was the only thing he still believed in. "Bailey, I—"

Like a bucket of cold water, the sultry sway of what I'd

always and forever think of as "our song" was ripped away, replaced by the electric chaos of "Footloose."

We jolted apart, our breaths jagged, our faces flushed.

"Alright. Ummm. Okay! Well, you all see how that's done," Knox said after a beat, but his gaze never left mine.

"Oh, we saw how it was done, son!" Blain said, and catcalled.

"Y'all need a moment or...?" Rafe called, earning a swift elbow from Sasha.

Greer fanned herself. "If that's how you *teach*, what must the final *exam* look like?"

"Anyway," Knox said. He strode over and killed the music. "So, we'll practice the Rumba later. Let's move on to the group dance, which will—"

"Wait. We're supposed to learn how to do that by *Saturday*?" Melody asked.

"Yes," Knox said, glancing at me as if he couldn't help himself. "Well, the dancing, I mean. The kissing is, ah, optional."

"But preferred!" Jessa called.

"Anyway," Knox said. "This is basically the same handful of steps over and over. Now, everyone line up and let's... make this look good for Jessa and Luke."

I nodded. I would try. But it seemed that my bones—my actual skeleton—had forgotten how to function.

WE DANCED ALL AFTERNOON—WHICH thankfully meant there was no time for the couples massage and makeover we'd won. *But it's fine!* Jessa had said. *You two live in Serenade Creek after all! You can come back and do it any time for date night! Fun!*

I tried not to look at Knox as she said it, knowing that wouldn't ever happen. But I'd met his eyes anyway and he'd offered me a smile that didn't show his teeth or meet his eyes.

Though the dancing actually turned out to be a blast, my muscles were screaming when I slid into the bubble bath. I'd taken twenty minutes to do some yoga, to try to stretch it out so I wouldn't be walking like the Tinman pre-oiling tomorrow.

Jessa had the genius—and welcome, for once—idea that Knox should get ready for our romantic dinner under the stars in Corey's room to give me privacy, so we could have a dramatic and swoony 'first look' at each other when we arrived at the table for two on the Starlight Terrace.

There was a garment bag hanging on the back of the bathroom door with a sticky note on it that said *WEAR THIS, BAILEY!* and I hoped it wasn't as, ah, loud as the dress she'd chosen for me to wear for the kissing contest. If I'd known she would be supplying so many of my outfits, I would've packed considerably lighter. I pretty much stuffed everything I owned into my duffel, having no idea what kind of attire I'd need.

I found myself singing as I did my hair and make-up, my heart pitter-pattering as if this was a real date.

I braced myself for the worst as I unzipped the garment bag but when I pulled out the dress, I smiled.

"Perfect," I whispered.

A little too formal for the occasion, maybe, but perfect.

It was a deep, moonlit navy with clean lines and a subtle satin sheen, elegant in its simplicity. It had a square neckline, barely-there spaghetti straps, and a low, scooped back. The skirt skimmed the floor, pooling just slightly at my feet, and when I moved, the fabric shimmered subtly. It was the kind of dress you wear when you don't want to look like you're hoping he'll fall in love with you—but you're definitely hoping he does.

I slipped into it and studied my reflection.

There were two new Eternal Roses in the vase and on impulse, I clipped them. I put one in my hair. Then I fished out a safety pin and some ribbon from my purse. Yes, I travel with arts and crafts supplies in my purse.

A few minutes later, with a final look in the mirror, I headed out to the west lawn.

I inhaled sharply when Knox came into view.

He was wearing a tux.

He smiled as I approached him and my dumb face broke into the world's biggest grin.

"Hey," I said.

"Hi."

We stood there for an awkward moment and then I hugged him. After a second's hesitation, he hugged me back. There was nothing awkward about it.

When we pulled away, I said, "So, you clean up nice."

What I wanted to say: *There has never and will never be a more attractive man than you.*

There was nothing, nothing, in this world I wanted to do more than be able to stare at Knox Showalter for the next two or three hours.

"You, too," he said. He made a face. "No. I mean. You're gorgeous, Bay."

"Why thank you, kind sir," I said. Thankfully I did not also curtsey and make it weird.

"Shall we?" he asked.

I nodded, suppressing my inner idiot, who wanted to say something along the lines of, *Oh, shall we ever!*

"Oh, wait, no." I held up the Enchanted Rose I was holding. "I made you a boutonniere," I said, suddenly shy. "If that's not too extra."

He blinked. "A boutonniere slash floral lie detector? Too extra? Nah," he teased. Then, slowly, he smiled. "It's perfect."

I took a deep breath and reminded myself that this was absolutely not a date.

"It's just a silly superstition," I reminded him, though, man, the thing with the wind blowing the flower out of my hair right after I claimed the peck I'd given Knox meant nothing was weird. Coincidental. But weird.

There are no coincidences in Serenade Creek, Cherish's oft-made claim floated through my head, buzzing like a bee.

Knox held still as I pinned it to his lapel, careful not to jab him.

"There," I said.

"I should've brought you a corsage," he said.

I shook my head. "A corsage is too close to being a bouquet for my tastes. This is enough," I smiled, pointing at the rose in my hair.

We walked over to the candlelit table and he pulled out my chair, then once I'd sat down, pushed it in for me before seating himself across from me.

"So, the Footloose dance is going to be a hoot at the reception!" I said, because don't all twenty-somethings regularly bust out the word hoot? "I mean, the choreography is amazing. I can't believe you've never taken a dance class. How did you even get into dancing? You're amazing!"

And I'm Bailey Cooper, walking, talking ego boost for men who already know she's too into them!

He shook his head. "Greer and her big mouth. I should really handcuff her and Corey together for blabbing about my sordid past."

"We don't have to talk about it if you don't want to." We could talk about the fact that we practically kissed each other's faces off in front of your friends, instead.

He chuckled. "No, it's okay. It's more funny than it is embarrassing now and I can't be mad about it since it was that talent show, actually, that got me into dancing. It wasn't supposed to be all me, by the way. Four of my buddies—not Luke—entered with me, but they conveniently didn't show up."

"Oh, no!"

Laughing again, he said, "Oh, yeah. And when they called our group up, everyone in the audience started chanting Knox, Knox, Knox!"

"Oh, no!" I said again. "Was everyone chanting Knoxley at the kissing contest a total nightmare flashback?"

"Actually, no. I wasn't thinking about anything but... I wasn't thinking about college. Anyway. Everyone thought I'd punk out, but I went through with it. All by myself."

"Do you remember the moves?"

He gave me a knowing look. "Not if you're going to ask me to do the dance for you."

"Did you win?"

"I came in twelfth place. There were thirteen acts. But... it was fun. So the next year, I entered again, this time with a group who did show up, and we did my original choreography... and took second."

As he spoke, he poured some ice water from the carafe into my glass, then his own.

"If at first you don't succeed, dance, dance again," I said, lifting my glass. He clinked his against it.

"To dance, dancing again," he said, but there was something so serious about the way he said it, as if he wasn't talking about the *Bye Bye Bye* talent show experience at all anymore.

He shook his head, as if to clear whatever thoughts were churning in there. "So, what did you order for dinner?"

Jessa asked me at lunch—after Knox had gone back up the room—what we wanted for dinner. I realized, with a slight jolt of panic, I had no clue what he liked to eat outside of the Summer Lovin' Festival food. I told her to double-check with him, claiming he was still deciding between a couple of favorites. I almost blew our cover with an "Oh, I don't know," but caught myself and redirected just in time.

"Oh," I said. "So, the caterers Jessa's using make these out of this world rosemary mashed sweet potatoes, so I couldn't resist those." I paused. "I should've suggested you get them, too. I'm sorry—"

"Did you do something wrong?"

"Well, if I let you taste the sweet potatoes? You will say that, yes, yes, I did something very wrong by not suggesting you have them, as well."

"Okay, fair," he said. "But you will let me taste them, though?"

"No," I said.

"Once again, fair."

I laughed. "I was joking. Of course I'll let you taste them. I'm not cruel. But was my no convincing, though?"

"Very." He smiled, but then he swallowed hard, his Adam's apple bobbing. He took a long sip of his water.

"Anyway, I'm having the rosemary mashed sweet potatoes with roast chicken and strawberry shortcake for dessert," I said. I glanced down at my dress. "I'm probably overdressed for roast chicken."

He shrugged. "I'm having pizza."

"You are not."

He nodded. "Spinach, mozzarella cheese and feta cheese, tomato slices. Yum. You'll tell me if I get spinach in my teeth, right?"

"I'll tell you by pointing and laughing," I teased. "Dessert?"

"Peach cobbler à la mode. Since moving to North Carolina, I have become totally addicted to peach cobbler and all things ala mode."

The server arrived with our food not long after that and we ate in companionable silence, other than the brief negotiations to trade four (heaping) spoonfuls of my mashed sweet potatoes for one slice of his pizza.

The candles were burning low. A breeze picked up, lifting the ends of the white tablecloth like it was trying to urge one of us to do something. Then, just like a scene change in a movie, slow music began to play from hidden speakers.

We both looked up. Then at each other.

He cleared his throat. Tapped his spoon on the rim of the empty cobbler bowl. Looked up at the stars.

"Do you..." I began. "Do you want to dance?"

He looked at me and... I couldn't imagine him saying anything other than yes.

CHAPTER FIFTEEN

BAILEY

But then he drew in a breath and took too long exhaling. Something twisted in my gut.

"It's okay," I said, before he could speak. "There's no audience. I get it. There's no reason to—"

"Bay. Bailey. It's not that I don't want to dance with you," he said. "It... I... We just probably shouldn't, not—"

"It's okay," I interrupted. I nodded, as Rihanna sang about having love on the brain. "It was a stupid suggestion."

I glanced at my watch, glad I'd worn it, even though it didn't go at all with the dress.

"Oh, wow. I'm supposed to meet Jessa, like, now."

"Huh," he said, looking down at his own watch. "She had something planned for you tonight? Right after our dinner? I would've thought she would've wanted to give us plenty of time to—"

"Yeah," I cut him off before he could spill just what he thought Jessa would've wanted to give us more time to do.

"She's just got so much going on. She probably forgot tonight was supposed to be my one-on-one toast with her. She's doing it with all the bridesmaids. I told her it wasn't necessary with me, since, you know, we're not friends, but..."

I was babbling and on the verge of absolutely losing it and he was looking at me like I was babbling and like he knew I was on the verge of losing it and it wasn't helping one bit.

I pushed my chair back with an unintended but obnoxious scrape that gave me a reason to wince. I so badly needed to wince. I stood. "Anyway, I have a champagne toast with Jessa. Like now. So I'm gonna go do that and—"

Knox stood, too. "Do you want me to walk you?"

That would only be slightly less awkward than my first boyfriend Wesley Connors driving me back home after the prom... where he dumped me.

"No, no," I said. "I'm meeting her on the back veranda, and... Yeah. I've got it. Thanks."

My legs were wobbly as I walked away.

I actually had half an hour before I needed to meet Jessa, but hopefully they wouldn't compare notes. I didn't really care if they did. I needed... I needed some time.

My hands wouldn't stop shaking, so I clenched them into fists.

I found myself headed towards the Fountain of Forever and I went with it, even though I felt just out of control enough to climb in and fish out all of the coins in order to make sure I retrieved mine, hoping this wasn't a no-take-backs situation.

When I got there, I sat on a nearby bench and listened to the water trickle and burble. It sounded like taunting.

"So, you kind of have a twisted sense of humor, don't

you," I said. "You bring me my soul mate, but he can't fall in love? You know him, right? Knox Showalter? The soul mate you sent to me? Unless you sent, like, Corey, and I've just been looking in the wrong direction?"

Yeah, I was unhinged. And I didn't care.

"Say something for yourself. You got anything other than the trickle and the burble?"

Oh, my gosh. I was five seconds away from throwing hands at *water*.

Maybe I should be concerned. Maybe I should try to reel it in.

The fountain blurred. But it wasn't magic. It was tears.

Angrily, I wiped at my eyes. "Say something for yourself. Am I wrong about it being Knox?" I whispered. I threw back my head and stared up at the vast, twinkling night sky.

And at that exact moment, a shooting star streaked across the black velvet.

I watched it in awe until it winked out.

Then I glared at the fountain.

I wagged my finger at it. "That was not you."

With a sigh, I heaved myself up and trudged to the veranda to meet Jessa.

Even though my watch confirmed I was still ten minutes early, she was already waiting.

"Bailey!" she called out, jumping up and rushing to sweep me up in a hug. "How was the dinner? I totally spaced and forgot it was your night, or I would've had you switch with Faye. I hate that I pulled you away from Knoxxy."

"It's okay," I said. "Dinner was lovely. Thank you so much."

"Well, you guys won it, fair and square," she said. "Come

on, let's sit over here. There's a super comfy loveseat. Can we chat for a few minutes before we toast?"

"Sure," I said, though my heart felt like it was simultaneously trying to crawl out of my throat and sink down into my stomach.

We got settled and then she said, "That dress looks amazing on you."

"Oh, yes! Thank you so much. It's gorgeous. You have great taste." Because it's not nice to tell someone they have hit or miss taste?

"Oh. Oh! He didn't tell you." She patted my knee. "I didn't pick this one out. Knox did. I figured he'd know your taste better than I would."

I drew in a deep breath that felt sharp around my lungs.

"It came from Wisteria Bridal Co., so Mabel had your size on file. I would never assume Knox knew that info," she laughed. "Luke certainly wouldn't, for me, and we've been together a ridiculous amount of time for me not to be wifed up already."

"Well, only a couple more days to go," I said.

She beamed.

"You guys have been together since college, Knox said?"

"Yeah. Fourteen years."

"Wow," I said.

"And now, you too are probably wondering why we're not married yet."

I shook my head. "Everyone has their own timelines."

And some of us are just cursed.

Giving me a small smile, she nodded. "Well. He'd been planning to ask me when Knox proposed to Stephanie. And then he didn't want to steal Knox's thunder, so we decided to wait until after they got married. And... well. Then it wasn't a good time. And I think he kind of got gun-shy after that, too. Like... would I do the same thing to him?" She shook her head. "What Stephanie did... none of us saw it coming. It threw everyone for a loop, to be honest. Anyway. Then my dad passed away. And... it took a long time for me to reconcile that he wouldn't be at my wedding to walk me down the aisle. We talked about eloping, actually."

"Why didn't you?" I asked. "I mean, not that you should've, but what made you change your mind?"

She grinned. Her eyes gleamed. "Luke, actually. It's so lame, but I'd kept these boxes and boxes... since I was a little girl... of pictures I'd torn out of magazines. Like a deconstructed wedding mood board. He found them and was like, nope." She deepened her voice, imitating Luke. "The woman I am marrying was once the little girl who filled up these boxes. We're having your dream wedding—nothing less. It's going to be perfect, if it's the last thing I do. Anything you want, baby. We'll make it happen." She laughed, ruefully. "I may have taken that a little too seriously."

I took a shaky breath. I understood a little better where Luke had been coming from, now, when he'd reached out to Cherish, at least. But, still, a twinge of guilt pinched my insides.

"I think that's a perfect segue to our toast!" she said. She got up. "Stay where you are. Tonight is about you, not me."

She walked over to a small table where the champagne was chilling, poured us each a glass, and brought them back. She handed me my glass and sat back down.

"Bailey," she said, smiling at me so warmly, so genuinely, so sincerely.

And this is why I could never do crimes, because one moment under interrogation with Good Cop would break me. They wouldn't even have to bring Bad Cop in the building, I would be confessing left and right to felonies and misdemeanors I didn't even commit.

"I have so much to be thankful for this week and I need you to know how thankful I am for you. I have so much to thank you for. I'd be remiss if I didn't start with what you've done for Knox," she blinked, and a couple of tears fell onto her cheeks. "I always knew my wedding would be one of the happiest times in my life. I had no idea a huge part of my happiness would be because Knox had found happiness again, too. Finally. I cannot thank you enough for that."

She paused. My intestines were actually squirming. I shifted in my seat, and tried to match her smile, but I know mine didn't reach my eyes. Like me, it was fake.

"I was concerned at first. I'll admit that. The fact that he kept you a secret from us all. That we didn't even know he was dating again, much less in a relationship. When we first met, I thought I was picking up weird vibes. Maybe I was just being paranoid." She took a deep breath. "But I was convinced you two were fighting. Terrified you'd break up and ruin my wedding."

Now she grinned at me, like we were in on some big secret. "But that's not going to happen, is it? I mean, obviously, you're not breaking up this week, but you're not going to, ever, are you? You two are the real deal."

I had never in my life wanted to just up and disappear so intensely. Not even after I caught the Eternal Bouquet for the fifth time and 500 pairs of eyes were on me.

I had never in my life felt so ashamed.

"Jessa—"

"No, no. It's bad luck to interrupt a toast and I will not have any bad luck this week," she chided, playfully. "I know we've just met, but honestly, I don't see a future where we're not besties. I have to be besties with the girl who made our Knoxxy fall in love again. And... I feel like a proposal is imminent so I want to get in dibs on Matron of Honor right now."

She laughed. I tried to join in but it came out *huh, huh, huh,* sounding kind of like I was reacting to being repeatedly poked in the side. She wasn't just envisioning my future with Knox—she was imagining it as part of her forever with Luke.

I tucked my free hand next to my thigh, clenched my fist, and dug my nails into my palms. I discreetly bit the side of my cheek.

"A week ago, you were a total stranger. But you stepped in and stepped up in a way no one I reached out to was willing to do. At the last minute. You have been a delight. You have fit in with our group like you've always been a part of it. You've been a good sport about everything and... at some point in the future, when I come to my senses, I'm sure I will apologize for at least some of it. So, thank you, Bailey, for being a part of my dream. For helping make this week, and my wedding, perfect. I was so afraid this week was going to be too hard for Knox. But I've seen so much joy on his face and... that's all you, girl."

She nodded at me, like it was okay for me to speak now, but I felt like there was a bowling ball lodged in my esophagus.

Her dream wedding, her perfect week, was a sham.

Because of me.

Because I'd agreed to this.

Because I hadn't shut it down from the start.

She raised her glass. I lifted mine, too, but as I did, she

pulled back, and I briefly panicked that she saw the deception written on my face.

"I can't lie to you!" she squealed and I almost jumped off the loveseat. "Ugh. Okay. You can't tell a soul this. Don't worry, Luke knows and I told Knox a couple of nights ago. I could never keep anything from them!"

It was like she'd scripted all this, or maybe fate had, to really stick it to me. I was already drowning in guilt. That dunked me under and held me there.

"No one else knows, though, not even my mom."

Can liquid quiver? Because I'm pretty sure my blood was.

"I'm pregnant," Jessa whispered, pressing her palm against her belly. "With all the other girls, I've faked the toast, just pretending to take a sip, but... Yeah. I had to tell someone I could trust or I was going to burst. I feel like you're a girl who can keep a secret."

Was she messing with me? She had to be.

But she wasn't.

Everything she said was true and pure and straight from the heart.

And that made it worse.

I wished she'd found us out and was playing with me like a cat with a mouse, trying to get me to fess up.

But she wasn't.

I cleared my throat. "Congratulations, Jessa! I'm so happy for you."

"It was taking us so long to get down the aisle I wasn't sure we'd ever get around to the having a family part," she said. "Needless to say, this was not planned. If it had happened a month earlier, I would be showing right now."

"Well, you're not. At all. I had no idea."

"Let's toast," she said, holding up her glass again. "You're supposed to have something old, something new, something borrowed, and something blue when you get married. I thought this," she touched her belly again, "was going to be my something new. But... here's to new life and new friends. I'm so glad you're one of my somethings new, Bailey."

She clinked her glass against mine. I don't drink. Ever. But I drank half the glass of champagne just to keep my mouth shut. If I didn't, I was afraid the truth was going to spill out.

CHAPTER SIXTEEN

KNOX

"I think we made a mistake," Luke said. I glanced at him, then at the six-foot-tall letters we were standing in front of—the word FOREVER spelled out in flowers, including some I recognized as Enchanted Roses.

He was tugging at his ear. Never a good sign.

I started walking and gestured at him to follow. I had seen no evidence that the Enchanted Roses actually wilted upon hearing a lie, but... if Luke needed to chat about the lie we were living, I wasn't willing to play it fast and loose with any of Jessa's photo shoot props.

"Hey," I said to Corey as we passed him. "Do not use that parasol as a sword."

"I wasn't going..."

I gave him a look. Yes, he was, and we both knew it.

"I promise I'll be a good boy. Please don't tell my mommy, Assistant Principal Showalter," Corey said, making his voice high and squeaky.

"Don't worry, I'll leave Greer out of this," I said, which earned me a gesture no *good boy* would make.

"Everybody watch out," Rafe warned. "I think that cardinal is trying to build a nest in the first R and Jessa will lose her mind if anybody gets bird poop on their fancy pants."

The cardinal. I shook my head. Now was not the time for birdwatching.

I picked up the pace and got Luke around the corner of the gardening shed, where no one could hear or see us.

He shook out his arms, from shoulders to fingertips. "Bro, I have regret sweat."

"Luke. Lucas," I said.

His eyes were wide with panic. "She's going to kill me. She's going to kill us both. If she ever finds out..." He sucked in a breath. "No. She won't kill us. She'll leave me. She'll leave me and I'll wind up like..."

"Like me." I filled in, as he started pacing.

His anxiousness was going to cause me to break out in regret sweat, too.

"Lucas!" I said, again. "Can you get control of yourself or do I need to slap you? Jessa isn't Stephanie."

"We should not have done this." He shook his head, still pacing.

"Hey," I said. "The more you move, the more you sweat."

"Oh, man." He stopped pacing. Turned around to face me. Lifted his arms. "My pits. Are soaked. Aren't they?"

Yeah, they were soaked.

"Okay, buddy," I said, walking over to him. "Let's just keep your arms down, okay? Arms down."

"Why did you let me go through with this?" he asked.

Then, as if he'd just realized it, he added, "We're lying to Jessa!"

"Okay. Okay," I said, trying to remain calm, because one of us had to.

"When she finds out—"

"She's not going to," I said. "We're almost there, bud. The wedding is tomorrow. We're going to get through this and Jessa never has to know."

He raked his hands through his hair, down his face. "I'm going to have to keep this from her our entire lives. Our entire lives, bro. Forever. We're starting our marriage with a crack in the foundation and I put it there!"

"Well," I said, shoving my hands in my pockets. "We could tell her the truth—"

"No!" he said. "Oh, no. No. She'll never forgive me."

"Okay, then," I nodded, trying to remain level-headed, but he was on the verge of hyperventilating and I wasn't far behind. "We'll stay the course. We're almost there. Bailey's doing great, right? We've got this. Let's just breathe and—"

"Bailey's doing too good!" he exclaimed. Pacing again. I mentally added *Find Luke some better deodorant and another shirt* to my To Do list. "Jessa came back from their toast last night going on about how you need to propose to Bailey *stat* because if you don't waste any more time, we could all raise our kids together and wouldn't that be amazing! Jessa loves Bailey. And that's a problem since she's the only one of us who does."

Doing everything I could not to picture a baby with Bailey's eyes, I looked down at my feet.

"Jess is going to be devastated when you two break up." Yeah, he hit me with air quotes.

"Well," I said, because that's all I had.

But Luke apparently expected more. "Well, what?"

I shrugged. Well was all I had.

"Well, you could actually, you know, date Bailey! Wind up happily ever after. We *could* raise our families together."

"Yeah, I don't think you paid Bailey enough to commit that much to the bit, my dude."

He looked at me, his expression serious. Too serious. "You like her. She likes you."

I couldn't deny it.

But when I'd tried to talk to Bailey last night at dinner, she'd fled like Cinderella at 11:59 p.m.

And she came back different. Guarded. Like while she was with Jessa, she'd built walls and didn't trust me to see behind them.

We were fully dialed in on fake dating. Might as well get the miscommunication trope on our real life rom-com Bingo card, as well. I could talk to her after the wedding. I *would* talk to her after the wedding.

That would give me more time to be sure, before I said anything to her.

Today, this week, wasn't about me. Us. It was about keeping my best friend from falling apart, getting him down the aisle in one piece.

"Are you gonna be okay, man?" I asked Luke. "What's really got you freaking out, because I don't believe it's Bailey being too good."

Yeah, Jessa would be disappointed when Bailey and I broke up, but not all couples last forever. Jessa's a grown woman. She gets that.

Luke sighed. "She was bummed about the photoshoot," he said.

I nodded, waiting on him to go on.

There had been a sunset photoshoot planned for this evening, but unfortunately, that's when the hot air balloon parade would be taking place. The rehearsal dinner was tomorrow night at sunset and on Saturday, the wedding was at sunset. We had run slap out of sunsets.

Reluctantly, Jess had moved the photoshoot to, well, now. We were just waiting on the ladies.

"I suggested we get the photographer to photoshop the sunset into the pics," Luke said. "No one will ever know, right?"

I cringed.

"She was not pleased. Said it would be a sham and was aghast—her word—that I would suggest such a thing. *Would you really be okay with any part of our love story being fake, Lucas?*" he asked, mimicking her. I added *Tell Luke to never do a Jessa impersonation again* to my To Do list.

"Oh, man."

"She cannot find out what we've done," he said.

I nodded, because, yeah. That would be bad.

"What have you done?" a voice asked and, yeah, I suddenly had a regret sweat problem myself.

We both turned and, yep, Jessa was standing there, arms folded across her chest and a high likelihood of smoke coming out of her ears.

This kind of thing didn't actually happen in real life... did it?

"What have you done that I can't find out about?" she asked. "What are you doing hiding behind the gardening shed?"

"We didn't hear your footsteps, babe!" Luke said. "You look gorgeous!"

He was speaking way too loud—one of his *I'm guilty*

tells. I could only pray that he would realize we didn't know how much she'd overheard—and would not volunteer any incriminating intel.

"Knox," Jessa said, turning to me. Tapping her foot. Eyes narrowed like she was trying to squeeze my head, because, yeah, obviously, as the best man, I was responsible for every misstep the groom took this week. "What've you done, sweetie?"

She only called someone sweetie when she's plotting their demise. It was one of her tells.

"We hired a live alpaca," I said. "To carry in the cupcakes for your bachelorette party."

"Two alpacas!" Luke said, pulling the front of his shirt away from his chest where it was kind of sticking now. "A backup alpaca. Just in case. Very classy."

Okay, yeah, ear smoke was definitely imminent.

"You hired barn animals? For my bachelorette?" she asked, blinking. "Our mothers are going to be there. Your nana is going to be there. It's supposed to be elegant!"

"We'll cancel the alpacas," I said. "No big deal, we'll just..." I pulled out my phone and scrolled. I think I accidentally gave a thumbs up to a text from the Hearts & Charts Brigade. "There. Canceled. No alpacas."

She looked from Luke to me and back again, then gave a slight shake of her head. "I would expect something like this from Corey. Not from you two. Why is your shirt damp?" she asked him.

I followed the two of them back to the FOREVER where the others had gathered. I stopped short when I saw Bailey.

It was my first time seeing her today—she was gone before I woke up this morning.

I drew in a deep breath.

She looked... luminous.

Her light orange dress was long and flowing, tied at her neck, her shoulders bare. Her hair was twisted up with a few curls trailing down her neck, and I had to physically stop myself from reaching out to trace the path of one with my fingers.

All of the ladies were wearing the same style dress, but in different colors. None of them pulled it off like Bailey.

Her gaze met mine. She smiled but... it didn't meet her eyes.

I walked over. "Is it a coincidence that my pants match your dress?"

Bailey wrinkled her nose. "A coincidence? On Jessa's watch? Never. You look good in faded tangerine, by the way."

"Is that what this color is?" I grinned at her. I couldn't control my face. "So do you, Bay. So do you."

There was a crown of Enchanted Roses in her hair, slightly off-kilter, and I reached out to adjust it. She pulled back.

"I was just straightening the—" I began.

"It's okay," she said. "It took like three hours to get this do done so... maybe don't touch it, though."

Don't touch me wasn't what she said, but...

"Hey," I whispered, but she'd turned away from me, was saying something to Melody.

She was upset about last night. Of course she was. She'd asked me to dance and I'd said, for all intents and purposes, no.

But if she hadn't bolted to go meet Jessa, I'd have finished my thought.

I hope I would've finished my thought. I hope I would've been brave enough

We probably shouldn't dance until after we talk.

That's what I'd been going to say.

Bailey Cooper, if I dance with you again, I might kiss you again and I can't kiss you again until we talk and are on the same page.

"Bailey," I said again, gently touching her elbow.

"What is it, honey?" she asked, looking back at me with a plastered-on smile.

It was subtle, the way she pulled back. Maybe not even conscious. But it hit harder than I expected. Like watching a door close slowly... and realizing it's been locked from the inside.

"I—"

"You all look amazing!" Jessa called. "I was upset about not having a sunset, but... you guys are my sunset."

"We look like we're about to be the chorus line in an off-off-Broadway musical," I whispered to Bailey.

She did not laugh.

The photoshoot started with enthusiasm and cheer—even if some of both were faked.

Bailey stood beside me, perfectly poised, every expression camera-ready—but she was stiff, guarded. She laughed when prompted, moved when told, turned her face to the light. But none of it was *her*. Not the Bailey I knew.

I tried to catch her attention between shots, but she seemed to be actively avoiding eye contact with anyone but the man behind the camera.

The poses changed every few minutes—arms looped, shoulders leaned, heads tilted. We were a carousel of fixed grins and fading patience. I checked on Luke whenever I could. I couldn't tell if he was trying not to pass out or not to pass judgement on himself. I gave him a quick thumbs-up. He blinked in return. Maybe it was Morse code for *I'm dying inside.*

Bailey shifted beside me. Her arm brushed mine. She didn't pull away, but she didn't lean in, either.

By the fifth pose, I was sweating. By the tenth, I could feel her dread. As we shuffled into place for what felt like the ninetieth pose, I'd run out of ways to silently tell her that I was sorry.

"Hey," I asked her. "Are you okay?"

"Yes," she said.

Her smile was strained, but by this point, all of our facial muscles were probably on the brink of collapse.

The overwhelming need to pull her aside gripped me. Not later. Not after the wedding. Now. I needed to tell her that when we'd kissed on the dance floor, I'd thought: This isn't fake. This feels real.

Then:

Why can't it be real?

And ever since...

Ever since, I'd been thinking that... maybe. Maybe I hadn't been unable to fall in love... maybe my heart had just been waiting to meet Bailey.

"Stop staring at me, please," she whispered, without looking at me.

"I'm fine," she said.

She wasn't fine.

She was aching and I could feel it.

"Hey," the photographer called. "Bridesmaid in orange—"

I could feel her every muscle tighten as Bailey tensed next to me. Everyone's attention swiveled towards us. Her.

"Something's going on with your flower crown," he said.

"Oh, yes," Bailey said, reaching up. "It's a little crooked, but I didn't want to..."

Her voice trailed off as she glanced at me and, I'm sure, saw my eyes widen.

"What is it?" she whispered, still frozen.

"It's..." My voice trailed off. I couldn't say what I was seeing, because I couldn't believe what I was seeing.

The Enchanted Roses were wilting. Drooping. Their petals curling in, edges withering.

Like they were fed up with the charade.

Like they'd gotten fed up with my lies, and hers, and had called us out.

"Oh, my word!" Jessa slipped out of the lineup and marched over, while all the other girls reached up and touched the flowers in their hair, peering at each other. I looked from Greer to Melody to Faye. It was as if the Enchanted Roses that made up their flower crowns were fresh off the bush while Bailey's had been sitting around for a few weeks.

"What's happening?" Bailey asked me, as Jessa began fussing with her hair.

"The roses went bad," Jessa said.

"What?" Bailey looked like she herself was about five seconds away from wilting under the scrutiny of all the eyes on her. "Knox?"

She turned to me, her eyes full of questions. Of panic.

"Don't worry about it at all," Jessa assured her. "The stylist probably just got too much hairspray on it. We have back-ups. Luke, can you—"

"I'm on it," Luke said.

"It's really not a problem," the photographer said. "I can fix it in editing."

"Jessa doesn't want the photos faked," Luke said. "I'll run get the—"

"Well, it would just be retouching, not... The thing is," the photographer said. "We only have about twenty minutes left and five more shots planned, so time is not on our side..."

"Hey," I whispered to Bailey. She was trembling and when I noticed it, it was like being punched in the gut. I put my arm around her shoulders, leaning in close. "It's okay. It's going to be okay. Twenty more minutes..."

"It's okay," Jessa said, with a decisive nod. "I trust you. I'm sure you'll do a great job and no one will be the wiser." She touched Bailey's arm. "It's not a big deal, okay? He'll fix it in editing. It's a fluke. Could've happened to any of us."

Bailey nodded, but as soon as Jessa's back was turned, she looked at me and I could read her thoughts.

This couldn't have happened to any of us.

It was like the universe had yanked the emergency brake. No more pretending. Not with the roses. Not with Bailey.

CHAPTER SEVENTEEN

BAILEY

I stood there with the telltale roses on my head and listened to Jessa remind everyone of the day's schedule. As soon as she was done, I excused myself and all but ran to the suite I'd been sharing with Knox. I couldn't look at anyone, not knowing that I was about to single-handedly ruin all of her plans.

The hot air balloon parade.

The unity dinner after.

The bachelor and bachelorette parties.

I wouldn't be there for any of it. I couldn't be.

And everyone would know the truth.

But I would be able to live with myself.

Hot tears burned my eyes but I blinked them back. I hadn't been able to resist the glance back over my shoulder at Knox. He hadn't followed me immediately, but he had watched me go, the same concern in his eyes that had been there all morning. He cared about me—I knew he did. So hopefully, even if we couldn't be together, he would understand what I had to do.

He would be here soon. I knew that, too.

Sure enough, as soon as I hauled my duffel bag onto the bed to begin packing, there was a light knock.

I turned and sat on the edge of the bed, ready to face him.

Not ready to face him at all.

But I had to.

He had to understand. He was Knox. He had to.

My stomach clenched. I swallowed hard, the taste of bile on my tongue.

"Bailey?" he called.

"It's your room. You can come in." I wrestled the flower crown out of my hair, not caring what I looked like now. The pictures had been taken. It didn't matter.

The pictures.

I should've done this before the pictures.

The door opened slowly and Knox stepped in.

Every time I looked at him this week, I felt a flush of warmth, and a little voice inside me whispering, Everything is going to be okay. I pushed it away before I could even really acknowledge it, not wanting to grow accustomed to something fleeting.

But I had felt it.

I didn't feel it now.

"Hey," he said, his voice low. He was still wearing the newsboy hat Jessa had put all the guys in for the photoshoot. He took it off, placed it on the nightstand. Smoothed his hair. Then, done with the busywork, he put his hands in his pockets, like he always did when he didn't know what to do with them.

I held up the flower crown—every single Enchanted Rose looking like they'd just, all at once, given up on life.

"So the jig is up," I said, and even though I tried to make it light, the words came out like a plate shattering on a tile floor.

"Just a silly superstition, right?" he asked.

The tears that had been threatening finally spilled over as I shook my head. "I don't think so," I said, as he blurred in front of me. I plucked off a petal. "We're liars." Another one. "We're liars."

"Hey," he said again, taking a few steps, closing the gap between us. He kneeled down in front of me. I held my breath as he reached up and wiped away my tears. I flinched when his thumbs brushed my cheeks, but I didn't stop him. I wanted to push him away. I wanted to pull him close. I didn't do either.

"I knew you were upset. And you have every right to be, but if you'd let me—"

"I'm not upset," I said, sniffling, feeling like a fool. I swiped at my eyes. "I'm mad."

His brow furrowed and he stood up, took a step back, looking at me quizzically.

"I don't cry when I'm sad. I cry when I'm mad."

I had always been the girl who bawled when she should scream. My throat tightened and my eyes glossed over, my power slipping away, my anger making me appear weak.

"Good to know," he said, which honestly just made me madder, because why was that good for him to know? In a few hours, he would be some awkward combination of a memory and an authority figure again. He didn't need an arsenal of fun Bailey Cooper facts.

But I said nothing.

He sat down on the bed next to me.

"You're mad at me, right?" he asked, after a moment.

I glanced at him. I took a shaky deep breath and let it out slowly. "A little."

He nodded. "I figured and—"

"I'm a little mad at you for not shutting this down from the get-go," I said and he opened his mouth but I shook my head. "I'm super mad at Cherish for agreeing to take this gig. I'm mad at Luke for dreaming this up. I'm really, irrationally mad at the bridesmaid who got in the fight with Jessa and dropped out two minutes before her wedding. And I don't even remember what her name was. But mostly? I'm mad at myself. Because... once again, I said yes when I should've said no."

"Bay—"

"I'm furious at myself," I said. I started mindlessly plucking petals off one of the roses on the crown. "I can't believe I agreed to this and I can't believe that I kind of let myself forget exactly what we're doing, until last night, when I was listening to Jessa. But I can't do this anymore."

I didn't say the rest. I didn't say that being around him made everything so light, so filled with joy... I'd just been sooo focused on him that... somehow... the gravity of what we were doing had slipped way off into my peripheral vision, until it was a blurry speck. Meaningless, almost.

"You can't..." he paused. "You can't... do what, exactly?"

I raised my brows and looked at him.

"Bailey..." he began.

I squared my shoulders, lifted my chin.

"Bailey, two more days. We've already gotten through the hard part—"

I laughed, a dry sound. "I can't believe you just said that,

Knox. We got through the part where we didn't know if we'd fool Jessa. But the hard part is going to be standing up with them and listening to them say *I do* and forever cementing a lie as a part of their marriage."

"Okay, but—"

I shook my head. "No. No buts. I can't do it. I won't do it."

"Bailey." He reached for my hand, the hand that wasn't clutching the telltale roses like they were a life raft. I pulled away.

"What are you doing?"

"I don't know," he said. "I just... I can't tell you how much I appreciate what you've done. How much Luke appreciates what you've done. And Jessa—"

"Jessa thinks I'm your girlfriend, Knox. She thinks we're going to be besties after this. But she's never going to see me again after the wedding, is she?"

"Bailey—"

I put the flower crown down on the duvet beside me and pressed my fingers to my temples. "Could you please stop saying my name and just listen to me? Please?"

"Yeah," he said. "Yeah, of course."

"If we go through with this, you and Luke are going to have to keep this from her forever, Knox. Forever. And if she finds out later, if she ever finds out, like, even on their 50th anniversary? She's not going to be like '*Oh, ho, ho, what a lark. I'm so glad you pulled that particular prank on me, honey!*' She's going to rewind their lives, through grandkids, through kids, through every single happy moment until she gets to this week. And she's going to scour their lives, wondering what else was lies. If he could lie to her about something this important... what else would he lie to her about? What other happy moments were just lies?"

I searched his face, begging silently for a flicker of understanding.

Agree with me, I pleaded silently. *You know I'm right. You know my heart.*

My heart that was crumbling to dust.

He said nothing.

Purdy purdy purdy.

Knox glanced away from me, out the window. I briefly hoped that he would open it so the pesky cardinal could just fly on in and poop on my head, giving me a reason to extract myself from this conversation fast.

I don't know what I had expected Knox to say, but I hadn't expected silence.

I folded my hands in my lap.

"They've gone to the airport to get their families," I said. "When they get back, we have to tell her."

"Bailey..." his voice trailed off. He shook his head. "Don't say your name, right. Listen. You're right."

It startled me. I looked up.

"You are." He nodded.

I sighed with relief. My shoulders slumped with it, my spine felt like it could bend again. "Oh, my gosh. Thank you."

"You're right about all of it. About what this will do to Jessa if she ever finds out. About the fact that I probably should've shut this down before it ever started. But I didn't."

I nodded. "I really believe if we come clean, if Luke tells her the truth, if we help him explain... she'll understand. I mean, she'll be ticked off. Apocalyptically so. But... ultimately, I think she'll see that Luke's heart... that our hearts were in the right place. That we were all trying to do a good thing."

"Or she'll call the wedding off, break up with Luke, and never forgive either of us," he said.

"Knox."

"I'm just saying. It's a possibility," he shrugged. He came back over and sat down beside me again. "I know what it's like to be dumped when you're supposed to be getting married, Bailey. I'm not trying to lay a guilt trip on you. I just... think about Luke having to go through that, and—"

"I don't think..." I began, but my voice trailed off. I didn't know Jessa. Not really. I had no authority to speak to what she might or might not do.

I looked at Knox. He wasn't saying anything, but his eyes were asking.

I closed my own eyes. Took a few deep breaths.

"If your mind is made up, your mind is made up," he said, quietly. "We'll just have to hope for the best."

I nodded. My mind was made up. "Thank you for understanding."

He shifted, hands clasped between his knees. "After this is all over, could we maybe... grab a coffee? Talk, before I leave for the summer?"

I wanted to say yes. But I couldn't. I was still Bailey Cooper, though—so I couldn't say no, either.

But being with Knox when I couldn't have him hurt too much. If we couldn't be anything more, the sooner we went back to strictly professional, the better for my heart.

Though how do you go back to being strictly professional after you've watched someone sleep? I tried to push away thoughts of this morning, when I'd laid in bed with Knox, not wanting to lay there and stare at him like a stalker but also not wanting to move and wake him. He'd looked so peaceful. Happy.

All my memories from this week would linger, like it or not. As they had last summer.

"I don't think we really have anything to talk about," I said quietly. "Do you?"

The *Do you?* had been rhetorical, so I wasn't upset by the silence.

I nodded.

Negotiations over.

Then he asked, "What if we *were* dating?"

It felt like my heart actually stopped.

I looked at him. "What?" I asked.

"If we were actually dating, would you stay? Could you—"

"What do you mean? If we were actually dating, of course I would stay. We wouldn't be faking anything. So there wouldn't be an issue. But we're not dating."

His whole face changed and I didn't like it. His expression was hopeful and it twisted something in my gut.

"But... we could be...?"

I was hearing things.

I had to be hearing things.

I popped up. Took off my sandals. Jessa's sandals. The sandals of the bridesmaid I'd replaced—whose name I didn't even know. Fished out a pair of my own shoes. Slipped them on and backed away from him.

"Bailey, wait. What if we weren't faking anything anymore? What if the only lies were when... and how... we became a couple?" His voice wavered when he said the words, as if even he couldn't believe what he was saying. As if he wanted to retract the offer before he'd finished making it.

I glared at him.

"Are you serious?" I demanded. "Did you seriously just —" I shook my head.

My mouth dropped open. I flexed my fingers and clenched them into a fist.

This time my tears weren't out of anger.

They were out of a sadness that felt like holding my heart under in an ice bath.

I'd been here before. So many times before. And I never would've thought Knox would be capable of this type of emotional sleight-of-hand. Love as a solution to something, not a promise of something.

"Really?" I asked, blinking. "I finally said no to something, Knox. After a lifetime of putting everyone else first. Of saying yes when I didn't want to. I said no. And you, of all people. The guy who saw me saying yes too much and called me out on it. You're trying to use my feelings to manipulate me into doing something I told you I don't want to do? How dare you dangle love in front of me like a carrot."

I covered my mouth with my hand, shaking my head.

He was on his feet, too, coming towards me. "No. It isn't like that."

"Don't," I said. "You've told me like 800 times that you can't date me. And now... now... now that it would get you something you want, you're..."

I couldn't even say it.

There was nothing quite as shattering as learning someone you admired, someone you thought was amazing, wasn't at all the person you thought they were.

"Bailey," he said.

"Stop saying my name!" I cried.

"Listen to me, please. This is incredibly bad timing, I know, but I wasn't trying to—"

There was a desperation in his eyes. He knew how bad he'd messed up. Good.

"I've been thinking—"

"I don't care what you've been thinking," I whispered. "Who are you, even? How could you?"

"I—"

I stalked to my duffel bag, shoved a few things in. "No. No. I can't…"

I had to go. I had to get out of here right this very second.

"Please let me explain."

I shook my head. I swallowed hard. My throat burned. "I'll get Cherish to refund Luke's money."

"Bailey, please let me—"

I shook my head again.

"No, Knox," I said. "You don't have to tell Jessa we were faking. They're your friends. If you want to, tell her I realized you are not the guy for me and ended things. You won't be lying."

"Bailey."

"Tell her I'm sorry," I said, as I walked to the door.

For reasons I didn't understand, because this was all fake, no *real* break-up had ever hurt me more.

CHAPTER EIGHTEEN

KNOX

I wanted to go after her. To try again to explain. To apologize.

But I didn't move. I sat with her final words, with her departure.

Her leaving was a no. A big one. And the best thing I could do—the first right decision in a week of wrong ones—was to let her have it.

You are not the guy for me, she'd said, but the way she looked at me when she said it. She'd wanted me to be. She'd wanted me to be and I'd stepped up at the worst possible time, voiced my feelings in the worst possible way. The hurt in her eyes... I'd put it there and I couldn't take it back. And she didn't want me to.

Bailey Cooper had walked away from me thinking I was trying to use her heart against her, and anything I did to convince her otherwise, at this point, would be the kind of manipulation she'd accused me of, wouldn't it?

Don't let her go!

That same voice had screamed at me last summer, when we said our final goodbyes at the Summer Lovin' Festival.

I hadn't listened then.

Don't let her go!

It was screaming at me again now louder than ever and I had to ignore it because the need I felt, to make her understand... it was for my own comfort as much as it was for hers.

I pulled out my phone and messaged Luke.

We gotta talk.

A response came through five seconds later.

Ooh. Sounds juicy. Talk about what.

Without a question mark. With a winky face emoji.

I blinked.

Luke didn't use emojis. Ever. He was pretty fanatical about using proper punctuation, though.

Was he choosing now, of all times, to mess with me?

Who is this? I typed.

The response: **Who do you want it to be?**

I closed my eyes. He was really on edge earlier. Was it possible he got drunk off mini liquor bottles in the limo on the way to the airport? I don't think he'd do that but, I really didn't need to add a buzzed Luke falling out of a hot air balloon to my list of potential upcoming catastrophes.

I raked a hand through my hair. As far as I knew, he was with Jess. If I called, she would hear every word, so I'd have to be careful. But texting wasn't getting me anywhere, so I had no choice. I took a deep breath. Hesitated. Then pressed the button with my thumb.

Someone picked up and there was laughter that wasn't Luke's.

"Melody?" I demanded.

"Hey, Knox, hey. What do we gotta talk about?"

"What are you doing with Luke's phone?" I asked, panic rising in my chest. "Did you ride with Luke and Jessa to the airport? Is he—"

"Why would I have done that? Who voluntarily goes to an airport when they don't have to?" she asked. "We're all down at the pool. You and Bailey should come down. Hang on."

Then it was Greer's voice. "YES! Knox. You two have to come swim with us!"

"Why do you guys have Luke's phone?"

"Bring Bailey down to the pool and we'll tell you," she said, laughing. "Oh, my gosh, Corey, do not splash me. I cannot get my hair wet!"

"Greer?" I asked, but I was talking to dead air.

Twelve-year-olds. Our friends were twelve-year-olds.

I stood up and paced.

One of the girls texted me again from Luke's phone:

Hurry. Bring towels!!!!!

And a bunch of laughing emojis.

Well. They might as well have fun while they can because things were going to get... bad.

And I'd just have to wait until Luke got back to talk to him.

Unless... I could call Jessa's phone and ask to talk to him...

But she'd hear in my voice that something was up.

No, I needed to wait.

He was going to lose his mind. Then Jessa was going to lose her mind.

Bailey was 100% right.

We had been so freaking stupid. So. Freaking. Stupid.

I flopped back on the bed, which maddeningly smelled like Bailey's perfume.

A wave of sadness washed over me.

I had been so freaking stupid.

And I could continue to be stupid.

I could wallow and wait, alone, and spin worst-case scenarios, letting Bailey's absence settle around me like a weighted blanket of regret.

"That's not who you are, Knox Showalter," I said. Wasn't I the assistant principal who was known for telling elementary school students it didn't matter if you couldn't do everything? The important thing was that you did something.

Now wasn't the time to wait and wallow.

Now was the time for my something.

Now was the time for a grand gesture.

An hour and a half later, all that was left to do was watch and wait.

I stood in front of the window-seat, which gave me a perfect view of the walkway leading to the grand entrance—and a perfect view of the cardinal who'd been following me around since I moved to Serenade Creek. Can birds get annoyed? If so... this one definitely was.

"I'm sorry," I said. "I know. I forgot to refill the seed in the feeder before I left home."

I shook my head, feeling ridiculous. Certainly this was not the same cardinal that had joined me on my patio every morning for my first cup of coffee.

"I..."

My voice trailed off before I could get into a deep conversation with my feathered friend. It would not be the first.

Jessa and Luke came into view, followed by their mothers, and Luke's father.

I raced downstairs, almost taking out Corey, who was coming up.

"Sorry, bro."

I slowed down once I was outside, because if I didn't, one of the mothers would certainly ask me why my pants were on fire. It felt like my pants were on fire. My pants, my hair, my life.

"Knox Showalter, you handsome young man!" Mrs. Griffith called as I strode out to them. She stopped walking and beckoned to me. "You come here right now!"

"How was the trip?" I asked, as Mrs. Griffith and Mrs. White flanked me like a pair of wings. They looped their arms through mine, resting their heads on my shoulder.

Jessa was beaming. Luke was fidgeting.

The sun literally hid behind a cloud.

My stomach turned over.

"Who cares about the trip?" Hilary Griffith said. "Knox! We are so happy for you!"

"So happy for you, sweetheart," Nadine White echoed.

Oh, no. Oh no.

I had been bracing to tell Luke that we had to tell Jessa the truth. I hadn't considered that they'd brought their mothers in on our ruse. But of course Jessa had told them.

Hilary and Nadine were practically second and third moms to me—each thinking they were the second—and were almost as invested in my love life as Serenade Creek's own Hearts & Charts Brigade.

"Your Bailey is amazing!" Hilary cooed.

My heart lurched at her name and then...

Why was Hilary speaking as if she'd met Bailey?

"The sweetest!" Nadine agreed.

What?!

I glanced at Luke, who gave me the world's most covert thumbs up.

I widened my eyes as much as I could without drawing attention to myself, hoping he would read it as a signal to give me more, but he just grinned.

"Uh... you all met Bailey?" I asked.

"Yes!" Hilary said. "She is a doll, Knox."

Nadine nodded. "Within three seconds, we could see how perfect the two of you are for each other."

"We'll be coming back for another wedding soon, won't we, love?" Hilary asked, waggling her eyebrows at me.

Luke's dad shrugged at me, like *What are you gonna do?*

My heart was pounding now. Bailey was still here?

Jessa's eyes had narrowed. Then she smoothed her expression and said, "She said she needed some air. I hope the girls weren't suffocating her. You know how Greer and Mel can be!"

"She must've slipped out while I was in the shower," I said. "I should go check on her."

Jessa nodded, slowly. "She's at the wishing pond, down by the main gates."

I forced a smile. "She loves the wishing pond."

"I don't know what else she would have to wish for," Nadine said, winking at me.

I hesitated.

On one hand, I really needed to fill Luke in.

On the other hand, I didn't want to fill him in and risk him ambushing Bailey—not until I knew why she hadn't left.

Jessa tapped her wrist, where a watch would be if she was wearing one. "We have to leave for the hot air balloon parade in one hour."

I nodded.

"A hot air balloon parade," Hilary said. "This place is so magical."

"I wish you guys could come," Jessa said. She looked at me. "Hey, Mr. Kissing Contest Winner… you don't think you could pull some strings and get them to let us bring a couple of extra—"

"Honey, no," Nadine said. "You kids go and enjoy. We'll be fine."

"I should go get Bailey," I said.

"Go get your girl, Knox!" Hilary said, punching me a little too hard in the shoulder. Well. She and Nadine would probably be tackling me to the ground so Mr. Griffith could pummel me once they found out what Luke and I had done, so… might as well get a head start on getting the hits in.

As soon as I was out of their sight, I took off running.

I stopped short when Bailey came into view. She was standing on the footbridge. She'd taken her hair down and it was curtaining her face as she looked down at the water. The sun had come back out and the wishing pond shimmered unfairly.

"Hey," I said, softly. She lifted her head and glanced up at me.

"So," she said. "Apparently I need to practice storming out more to perfect the art." She sighed. "I haven't changed my mind."

I held up my hands, as if to say *I come in peace.*

"I'm not going to try to get you to change your mind," I said.

I sighed, too.

"Bailey..." I began, then swallowed the rest of my words.

There were so many things I wanted to say to her, but if I'd proved anything to her, to myself, it was that my timing was horrible. If I said any of the many things I wanted to say now... it would look like I was trying to get her to change her mind, or worse, to lay guilt on her she didn't deserve.

"What's going on?" I asked her, keeping my voice light.

And I waited.

Because right now... Bailey didn't need me to say anything.

She needed to be heard.

Deep in my gut, I knew that. And I didn't need to tell her that I would spend the rest of my life listening, if that's what it took to get her to trust me again. I needed to show her.

She took a deep breath and exhaled. She turned and leaned against the rail, facing me. With a self-deprecating smile, she said, "I said no. I stood up to you. I stood up for myself. And then I puked in the bushes." She pointed. "And then I held my head high. I straightened my shoulders, and I marched towards the gate."

I shoved my hands in my pockets. "Okay."

She didn't say anything else.

I waited.

Finally, she laughed. "I marched toward the gates and I remembered that Cherish—you know, my friend Cherish who is probably going to hate me—drove me here. I left... but I have no way to leave."

I waited.

"Yeah. So. I was just standing here, at the wishing pond, the useless, useless wishing pond, wishing that, I don't know, a horse-drawn carriage would happen by to whisk me away or I had the courage to steal one of the golf carts, because, yeah, I considered that. Or, you know, that I'd just disappear."

She wasn't finished.

I waited.

"I did not disappear. No carriage happened by. I met Jessa and Luke's parents, though," she said. She squeezed her eyes closed. "I texted my friend Lyric. She'll come get me but can't be here for another hour. We should really talk to the mayor because it's crazy that rideshares aren't allowed in the city limits."

She hung her head again.

I gave her another minute or two of silence, just to make sure she wasn't going to say anything else.

"Come on," I said.

She peeked up at me. "I can't go back there, Knox. I can't—"

"We're not going back," I said. "I have my car." I took out my keys and jangled them. "I'll be your getaway driver."

She tucked some hair behind her ear, confusion sweeping across her face. "What?"

"Or you can take my car," I held the keys out to her. "Drive yourself home. We can figure out how I can get it back later."

"You're not... you're not going to try to get me to change my mind?"

She sounded almost disbelieving. Like she'd been bracing for another fight, and was confused that I was giving her, without argument, what she needed.

I shook my head. "Nope."

"But—"

"I need to talk to Luke. Soon. Tell him what's happened. Help him make things okay with Jessa." I took a deep breath, exhaling it slowly.

"I should come with you. For that. I should—"

I shook my head. "There are no shoulds here. This is a should free zone, Bailey Cooper," I smiled at her. I wanted to walk over to her, take her in my arms, hold her. But I didn't. What she wanted mattered more than what I did. "They will be okay, Bailey. Or they won't. But... none of this... none of this is your responsibility. He was already feeling guilty. Having some second thoughts about lying to her. This is the right thing to do."

"But I..."

"Do you want me to drive you home or do you want to take my car? Either way is fine with me," I said. Then I added, hoping she would understand that I wasn't just talking about which way she was going to choose to leave the Enchanted Rose. "Whatever you want, Bailey. Whatever you want."

She took a few steps towards me.

"You don't have time to take me," she said. "The hot air balloon parade... I don't want Jessa to miss it and... Maybe I should wait. We can tell her after?"

I closed the gap between us. I took her hand in mine. I pressed my keys into her palm.

"Go."

"My duffel..." she said. "I... hid it in that bush." She pointed and started to walk towards it.

"I'll get it," I offered.

"That's not the bush I puked in."

I nodded. I walked over, dragged it out, hoisted it onto my shoulder. "What is in this thing?"

"Every pair of shoes I own," she said.

"I'm in the back parking lot. Come on," I said.

There was so much I wanted to say to her. But right now... the right thing to say, the only thing to say, was to reassure her that it was okay for her to leave.

So when she looked at me, with those big eyes, and whispered, "I'm sorry, Knox," I shook my head and whispered back, "You don't have a thing to apologize for, Bailey Cooper."

I did. And Luke did. But she absolutely did not.

"What do you mean, she's gone?" Luke tugged at his ear.

"She left," I said, again.

"I know what the words mean, Knox! But..."

He turned in a slow circle, craning his neck, looking around as if the answers he was seeking might drop out of the sky. Or if Bailey might be hiding behind a topiary.

"Please, please," he said, facing me again. "Please tell me this is a prank, and Bailey's about to pop out from a bush and tell me this was all a joke..."

He shook his head. Closed his eyes.

"Knox. Don't do this to me, man. Please don't do this to me."

"She can't do it."

"She has to. She has to. She has to!"

"Okay, okay," I said, clamping my hand on his shoulder. "You can say it as many times as you need to, but it's not going to change anything. Bailey is out."

"No," he said, his voice hoarse. He opened his eyes. Looked at me. Pleading. "She can't be out. You know where she lives right? Go get her. She really likes you. I know it. You can talk her into..."

I shook my head. "She's out, dude."

"But that means..."

He paled.

I nodded. "We have to tell Jess."

He shook his head. "No. No. Knox. I've never asked you for anything, man. Please. You can get Bailey to come back. Jessa never has to know."

"Hey," I said, moving my hand to his neck, giving it a light slap. "Listen to me. Bailey is right. This whole plot... Your heart was in the right place. I get what you were trying to do. But I should've told you no the second you told me your plan. Because I'm your best man. But I'm more than that. I'm your best friend. And I should've told you this was ridiculous and it would not work and even if it did, it wasn't worth the price you'd have to pay."

"Knox—"

"For the rest of your life, man. Bailey is right. And you know it. You already knew we were making a mistake. You were already second-guessing this."

He was breathing heavily. Sweating. Looking clammy.

"There's a bench behind you. Sit."

He collapsed onto it.

I sat down next to him.

"I can't tell her," he whispered. "I can't..."

"Well, the alternative is to hope that she doesn't notice she's down a bridesmaid again, but as detail-oriented as Jessa is—"

"Are you joking right now? I may be having a coronary, and you're bringing me jokes?" He moaned. "We were so stupid."

"So stupid," I agreed. "But Jessa knows us. She knows we can be stupid. It'll be—"

"She's going to call the whole thing off. She's going to..." he dropped his face into his hands. "It's over. It's over."

"Hey." I smacked him—not so lightly—on the shoulder. "It is not over. Listen to me. I let my... I've been carrying around baggage for far too long and I've let it... no, I've made some very bad decisions because of it. I'm done— we're done—letting what Stephanie did cloud our judgement."

He looked at me.

"I do have feelings for Bailey. I might... love her."

"I knew it," he said.

"I messed things up," I confessed. "Really bad. But... right now, right now, we have to focus on Jess. She isn't Stephanie, man. Stephanie was never going to marry me. Jessa wants nothing more than to marry you. She's waited so long. You both have. You two are not me and Stephanie. Jessa's going to be ticked off, but... she loves you. I don't think anything you could do will change that."

"She is going to scream."

"Mm-hmm."

"She's going to cry."

"Yep."

"She's probably going to kick both of our butts."

"And we deserve that," I said, and nodded. "But she will

marry you, Luke. She's going to marry you. Saturday. And you're both going to get a marriage that's not built on a lie."

He exhaled and it looked like a balloon deflating. But then he sat up straight. Nodded. "Jess deserves that."

"You both do."

"Okay," he said, slapping his thighs. "I guess I'll go... tell her. Probably shouldn't do it on the balcony, right?"

"Actually..." I stood, too. "Follow me. I know the perfect place."

"What..."

"Just come on," I said.

When we got there, he stared at me.

"Did you and Bailey..." He shook his head, looked at me, then back at the letters, confused. "I already forgive you, man. You didn't have to—"

"No," I said. "Bailey and I didn't do this for you, my dude. I did this, for you, for Jessa."

I'd taken the letters that spelled FOREVER, brought over some letters from where their names—JESSA & LUKE GRIFFITH—were spelled out by the pool, and rearranged them to spell FORGIVE US.

"There was no M, so I couldn't do FORGIVE ME," I explained. "But... US is probably more fitting, anyway, since you were not alone in your transgressions."

"No offense, bro, but... this is lame. This is not going to—"

"Fix things?" I interrupted. I shook my head. "It's not meant to fix things. Of course it's not going to fix things. And yeah, to you, it may look lame. But think about it. This," I gestured at the six-foot-tall floral arrangements. "This is her love language. It says: we see you. We know you. We love you."

He gave me a skeptical look, then one corner of his mouth lifted in an almost-smile. "This is my girl," he said. "Can you go get her? Send her out?"

"That's the least I can do," I said.

CHAPTER NINETEEN

BAILEY

"Bailey, Bailey, Bailey!"

I was home.

I should've been home-free.

But alas...

Before I could twist my key in the lock, the door to the apartment across the hallway opened and there stood Stanley.

My neighbor Stanley.

Hearts & Charts Brigades' Stanley.

"Hi, Stanley. I was just—"

"You did it, my girl!" he said. "You did it."

I glanced over my shoulder to see him pump his fist.

"Uh... I didn't do anything," I said, as politely as possible.

"He's good," Stanley said. "I'll give him that. The boy is good. Going on about how he wasn't interested in any kind of romantic entanglement, now or ever. Had us all fooled—"

Against my better judgment, I turned around to face him. "Hey, Stanley, I—"

"Cornelia is having a minor breakdown over the fact that there was a couple right under our noses and none of us had any idea! She'd taken you off the spreadsheet, miss, but I knew..." He wagged his finger at me. "*I knew*. I sat at that table with Knox just last Friday and I saw him looking at your table and I knew. Well. I didn't know obviously, because no one did. You two were so covert! And making it public at the kissing contest! Inspiring!"

"Stanley—"

"How long have you two been a thing? I won't tell Cornelia or any of the other ladies. I promise. I just want to know for my own knowing. We all thought the Eternal Bouquet was broken. That it had stopped working. But you had us fooled! It just knew better than us all! Have you two been together all along? Since last summer? You have, haven't you? You met him right after you caught the bouquet that first time and—"

"We're not together, Stanley," I blurted.

He looked like he'd just witnessed me tell him unicorns were real and then saw me punch one in the face.

"What?"

"Knox and I aren't a couple. It was just a kiss," I said. "To raise awareness for... Never mind. I'll... see you later."

I slipped inside my apartment. Closed the door behind me. Kicked off my shoes. Put on my favorite ratty as heck PJs.

I went to the freezer and pulled out a pint of ice cream. Grabbed a spoon.

Flung myself down on the couch.

After the first bite, I put the ice cream down on the

coffee table, placing the spoon on its lid. Strawberry cheese-cake had always been my favorite flavor, but all I could think about was Knox, last summer, offering me a bite of his cone. This pint was fresh, but it tasted freezer burned. It tasted like sweet, sticky regret.

The refrigerator was too loud. The air conditioner sounded judgey. And there it was again—that soft purdy purdy purdy from outside the window.

"Are you gonna nag me forever, buddy?" I asked.

I clicked the TV on and flipped through all the channels.

Why was there never anything on?

I was itchy. Restless.

I knew it would be this way.

I'd done the right thing.

But...

Jessa was going to be so disappointed.

Ultimately, she'd get over it. She and Luke would be fine.

But what he and Knox had done... what we had done... would always taint her memories of the ceremony. And I was in the pictures. She'd never be able to look at them without...

No.

I had made the right decision.

I was going to feel uncomfortable. Of course I was. Because I was letting people down.

I sighed.

I needed to text Cherish. To let her know I put the bail in Bailey. To tell her to refund Luke.

My stomach churned at the thought of it.

She was going to be so mad.

I swallowed hard.

Pulling out my phone, I opened my texts. I hadn't really looked at them since the kissing contest.

Two hundred.

Two hundred unread messages blinked up at me.

I texted Lyric to tell her I was home and didn't need a pickup from the Enchanted Rose after all.

Then I began scrolling. Doomscrolling.

The elementary school receptionist, Mrs. Wyatt, still hadn't found a summer home for the school mascot, Hammy the Hamster, and wanted to know if I could keep him again this year.

Nope.

Jocelyn Stillwell, the music teacher, had sent me a message to remind me about Piepalooza and another message expressing her shock about me and Knox: *We had a faculty-wide agreement that none of us would date him! Where's your solidarity, sister??? Some things are off-limits.*

"You're married, Jocelyn," I muttered. "Why do you care?"

Also: I had no idea what she was talking about. It's possible there had been a staff luncheon where everyone declared their loyalty to each other and decided as a group that none of them would date Knox out of solidarity. But if such a luncheon had happened... they obviously didn't need egg salad, which is probably why my invite had been forgotten.

There were messages from my friends, including so many from Cherish asking how it was going. Messages from parents of my students. Messages from... basically everyone who lived in Serenade Creek. I'd been added—along with Knox—to a group text with the Hearts & Charts Brigade.

I was about to open my notes app and draft a message to Cherish when Kelsie texted.

These are going to be on the front page tomor-

row. I am so sorry! If I wasn't in Montana, I would stop it. Also... is there something you need to tell me????

She'd attached pictures. From the kissing contest. There were two of me and Knox.

I sucked in a breath.

It was after we'd kissed.

He was looking at me. Stunned. But also...

I closed my eyes.

I'd seen him look at me.

I'd been right there.

But I'd been stunned, too, and...

There was something about seeing it through someone else's eyes.

He was looking at me like... like I was something precious. Like he was seeing me for the first time and the millionth. Like...

No.

Knox Showalter isn't who I thought he was.

I wiped at my eyes. Angry tears filled them.

What if we weren't faking anything anymore? What if the only lies were when... and how... we became a couple?

"How could you, Knox?" I whispered.

Hadn't he understood? If he'd just asked me to stay—just said please—I probably would've. Wouldn't I? I probably would've gone through with it, simply because I wouldn't have been able to say no to him? But he'd...

I shook my head.

No.

No. If I was thinking about myself right now, I wasn't the person I thought I was either.

Across town, Knox and Luke had probably already told Jessa the truth by now.

It was the right thing to do. I was sure it was the right thing to do.

But had leaving been?

Jessa had trusted me. Welcomed me. Treated me like a friend.

"No," I said, out loud this time, like I needed to hear it as much as say it.

This wasn't about regret. Or guilt. Or even Knox.

This was about showing up. For Jessa. For what was right.

I grabbed my shoes.

I didn't know if I could forgive Knox. Or myself.

But that didn't change the fact that...

After what we'd done, the least we could do was give Jessa the right to choose.

She'd wanted a bridesmaid she could count on to fill in for the one who'd dropped out. For the friend who'd turned her back on her.

And I'd done the same thing.

No.

I had to go back.

Not for Cherish.

Not for Knox.

Not even for myself.

Not because I'm *Bailey Always Says Yes*.

But because Jessa deserved the wedding of her dreams. Even if we'd made it tangled and messy and far less than perfect, I could help turn it around. I could give her my presence. I could keep her numbers even, if nothing else.

If Jessa still wanted me... If Jessa still would have me, I

would fulfill the duties I'd agreed to. Not as Knox's girl-friend. But as her friend.

Maybe one day, we'd laugh at how we met?

"Or... maybe not," I said.

I glanced out the window.

Maybe I could make it back for the hot air balloon parade. If I hurried.

I raced out the door, glad I hadn't had the energy to lug my duffel bag to the apartment and had left it in Knox's car. There wasn't time to change. There wasn't time to think. Just enough time to hope I wasn't too late.

CHAPTER TWENTY

KNOX

It was quiet. Too quiet.

I wasn't trying to eavesdrop, but I stayed close—close enough for the fallout—after I walked Jessa to Luke.

She'd looked from me to him and she took in the floral letters that spelled FORGIVE US.

Luke had gestured at me to go.

"What's going on?" I'd heard her ask.

But nothing since.

Not a shriek, not a yell, not a sob, not a swear.

I checked my watch.

Five minutes passed. Six. Seven.

Then she came around the corner and would've crashed into me if I hadn't stepped out of the way.

"Knox Showalter, you idiot!" she cried.

"I—"

Luke trailed behind her and he didn't look devastated, so... maybe that was a good sign?

"Is... everything okay?" I asked.

"No, everything is not okay. Did you not just hear me call you an idiot?" Jessa shook her head. "Bailey's really not your girlfriend?"

I glanced at Luke.

"Don't look at him. This isn't an open book test. Just answer me. Don't try to get your stories straight. Just tell me the truth, Knox."

I swallowed hard. "I'm really sorry, Jessa. Bailey and I aren't together. We aren't dating. She's not my girlfriend."

"Then she's an idiot, too!" she cried, throwing her hands up.

"Hey, listen, so I understand that you're upset, but Bailey isn't—"

"Oh, I'm upset alright." She rolled her eyes. "But I'm not upset for the reason you think I'm upset."

I glanced at Luke again.

Jessa grabbed my chin. "Do not look at Lucas. Look right here. At me. I'm not upset that you and the big dumb man I love hired someone to pretend to be my bridesmaid."

"You're... you're... not?" I stammered.

"No. I am not." She laughed. She actually laughed. "I have been such a control freak Tasmanian devil of a bride. It doesn't surprise me that you two did something so... so... nutty... in the name of keeping me happy. Now, had you actually gone through with it... yeah... we would be having a very different conversation right now. But thankfully Bailey put on the brakes when she did."

"She's—"

"She's an idiot. Just like you. Just like Luke," Jessa shook her head. "Knox." She put her hands on my shoulders. "That kiss. That kiss at the kissing contest. That kiss on the dance floor. Those kisses were *not* fake."

"I..."

"They weren't fake, were they?"

I looked up at the sky. Back at her. "I don't think so, but—"

"And the story about the two of you, how you met? At the Ferris Wheel? All of that was true, wasn't it?"

I nodded. "Well. Not the part about us having been together ever since. It was just a week. It was never supposed to be more than that."

She shook her head. "Oh, yes, it was. From the moment you met Bailey Cooper, it was supposed to be forever and nothing you can do or say will convince me otherwise."

"Jessa."

"It was, Knoxxy." She stared me down. "You love that woman."

"Jessa."

"You love that woman and she loves you," Jessa grinned.

I hadn't even admitted it to myself until that moment. But she was right. At least half right.

"Go get her. Bring her back here," Jessa commanded.

"I..." I spread my hands, helpless. "I messed up. She left. I don't want to ask her to—"

"She left because she didn't want to pretend, Knox! Not for me and not with you!" Jessa cried.

I glanced at Luke.

"We can change the letters to say *Date Me For Real?*" he asked.

I glanced at Jessa, who was obviously doing the mental math on whether or not that would actually be possible, with the letters available.

"If she doesn't want to be a bridesmaid for me, that's fine," Jessa said. "I mean, I want her to be. Make that clear. I really, really want her to be. But... if she doesn't want to be, I understand. However... I will not understand if she doesn't come as your plus one." She slapped me on the shoulders. "She's going to be your girlfriend and she's going to be my friend. Go get her, Knox Showalter."

My heart was beating way faster than it should be.

I bit my lip.

"I'm going to go get her," I said, and I meant it, even though the words sounded far-fetched and ridiculous, like I was announcing I'd lasso a star and shimmy up to the moon.

I started backing away from them.

"I'm going to go get her!" I shouted.

"Yeah, you are!" Jessa cheered.

"We probably won't be back in time for the hot air balloon parade!"

"Probably not, unless you plan on getting her back here by shouting *I'll explain later!* as you toss her in the trunk of your car," Jessa said, rolling her eyes.

"Why don't you take the moms in our place?" I called over my shoulder, as I started to run.

"Yes! They'll love it. Go, go, go. I better look down and see you and Bailey kissing!" Jessa called.

I lurched to a stop, skidding a bit. "I don't have my car!"

"What?" Luke asked. "What do you mean you don't have your car?"

"Where is it?" Jessa craned her neck and looked around as if it might be misplaced, having gone rogue and parked itself behind one of the topiaries.

"Bailey took it!" I threw my arms wide.

Luke's mouth dropped open. "Bailey stole your car?"

"Of course she didn't. Shh," Jessa smacked him lightly across the stomach. She was clearly thinking. "We'll need the van to get to the hot air balloon parade or I would let you... Take one of the golf carts!" Jessa exclaimed. "They're parked out front!"

"Yes!" I cried, like she'd just told me I won five million dollars. She was clearly giddy and I was getting swept up in it. "Yes! The golf carts! I'll..."

"What?" she asked.

"I don't know where she lives!"

Jessa did a double take. "But I thought you lived in the same building? Oh, my goodness. That was a lie, too? Do they have reform school for grown men, because I think you two—"

"Never mind!" I said. "I'll figure it out."

I raced toward the main gate. No, I didn't know where Bailey lived. But I knew someone who probably did. And thankfully he'd texted me no less than eighteen times since the kissing contest, so I had his number.

"Stanley!" I blurted when he answered on the third ring. "How are you, man?"

I climbed into the golf cart like it was a getaway car, turned the key, and floored it out of the Enchanted Rose Inn grounds like I was escaping a crime scene.

Except "flooring it" in this thing meant hitting twelve miles per hour going downhill.

"Knox Showalter! Well, well, well. All of my messages are still on unread so I thought you were avoiding me—"

"Hey, no, not at all. Well, maybe a little bit," I said, because enough lies, right? "Sorry about that. It's just that everyone in town, more or less, has been blowing up my phone this week. Hey, tell me, do you know where Bailey lives?"

"I do," he said. "I just saw her actually and Knox, I was saddened when she told me you two are not an item yet."

She told me you two are not an item yet...

Had she said *yet?* No, that was probably a Stanleyism. Just like use of the word item.

"Wait," I said. "You saw Bay? Bailey?"

"I did. She lives in the apartment across the hall from me," he said.

I'm not saying I believe in fate, but... what are the odds?

"Where? What building?"

"Maplewind Court. Apartment 211. That's her. I'm 210—"

"Thanks, Stanley. Talk to you later—"

"Wait a second, Knox—"

"Thank you so much!" I said and ended the call. I couldn't risk announcing to one of the Hearts & Charts Brigade that I loved Bailey—did I?—and having everyone in Serenade Creek hear it before I had the chance to tell her.

A squirrel darted into the road, froze, and looked at me like *I* was the problem. I swerved, veering halfway into the other lane to miss hitting him.

"Sorry, buddy!" I called, glancing up as a car came around the curve from the opposite direction. Going fast. Too fast.

I laid on the horn, fully expecting a shallow and ineffective *meep meep* but no, it was wedding bells so loud I jumped in my seat. I jerked the wheel, yanking the golf cart back into my own lane—causing it to teeter.

The other driver slammed on the brakes. Tires shrieked.

Her eyes were wide.
So were mine.
It was Bailey.

CHAPTER TWENTY-ONE

BAILEY

I rolled down the window.

"You were in my lane!" I shouted at Knox.

My heart was pounding.

"I know," he said, holding up his hands in surrender. "I'm sorry! Are you okay?"

"I almost annihilated you!" I cried, rubbing my shoulder where the seatbelt had dug into it.

"I probably deserve annihilation right about now," he said. "Can we talk?"

So I can tell you it hurts to look at you?

"Are you serious right now? I actually could've killed you, Knox. We need to get out of the road," I said.

He nodded. "Let's pull over and—"

I shook my head. "Not here. I was going back to the inn."

The hopefulness in his eyes tugged at my heartstrings.

Remember what he did, Bailey. Stay strong, girl.

But all I could remember was his laugh when we were

hanging out in the room between wedding events as he insisted I show him some yoga poses. So he could be smoother on the dance floor...

"I am going back for Jessa," I said, my voice far more resolved than my heart. "If she still wants me—"

"She does," he said and the idiot got out of the golf cart, leaving it right where it was, without even pulling off onto the shoulder.

"Knox—"

He walked over. "Luke and I told her everything, Bailey. She still very much wants you in the wedding. But only if you want to be. She wants to be your friend, still. Whether you're a bridesmaid or not. Whether you say yes or not."

I let out a relieved sigh.

I wanted to ask the very Baileyest question of all: *Is she mad at me?*

But I swallowed it. It didn't matter. Jessa had every right to be mad at us all.

But she still wanted me at the wedding.

So there was still going to be a wedding.

That meant she planned on forgiving Luke, right?

That was the only important thing.

"I was actually coming to tell you," he said. "She ordered me to come get you back. I... I wasn't going to come after you. I wanted to. But I wanted to respect your wishes. That was the most important thing to me. That you felt heard."

We really needed to get out of the road, but I had to sit with that for a second before I could say anything.

"I'm going back for her. Not for you," I said. I didn't say it meanly—but I needed to say it.

"Bailey, what I did. What I said—"

"Knox." I shook my head. Looked away from him. Kept my eyes on the road.

"I owe you an apology. And... if and when you're ready for it... I'd like to give you an explanation, as well."

Adrenaline was still coursing through me from the near miss collision. My hands were shaking. I wrapped my fingers around the steering wheel and squeezed it tight.

"Meet me back at the Enchanted Rose," I said.

"Bailey—"

I glanced at him. So handsome. So everything I thought I'd wanted for the past year.

"You hurt me," I said.

"Bailey, I know, and there are not enough *I'm sorrys*—"

"Let's talk back at the inn," I said, and rolled the window up.

I didn't know what I wanted to say. What I wanted him to say.

But I had time to think about it. A turtle with a limp could've beaten Knox back to the Enchanted Rose. I went up to the room and changed clothes—thankfully only a bellhop saw me in my ratty PJs—but I didn't want to wait there. Not where I would keep replaying that last conversation we'd had and keep festering in that hurt.

I went to the one place I knew I would see him coming back in—the Fountain of Forever.

He finally showed up, hair windblown from the ride, tie askew, cheeks a little pink.

When he spotted me, he slowed.

"I'm going to move my stuff to Corey's room. I can sleep on his couch. He still has one."

I shook my head. "You don't have to. Since the truth is

out, I think Jessa will understand me spending the last couple nights at my own place."

He raised his brows. "You have met Jessa, right?"

We both laughed, but it was forced.

"Do you feel like talking now?" he asked, after a moment.

I nodded. Talking now felt like the most important thing in the world, because if this week had taught me anything, it was that, whether it's pleasant to hear or not, the truth matters.

"I..." he began, but then he laughed again, nervously this time. "Can I take a minute to gather my thoughts? I don't want to mess up again."

He began pacing.

I watched and waited with nervous nausea, the words *would you hurry up* burning the tip of my tongue.

Back and forth, back and forth.

Then he bent down.

Picked up something.

And casually tossed it into the fountain.

"What did you just do?" I blurted.

He glanced at me. "There was a quarter on the ground."

Oh. My. Stars.

"There was a quarter on the ground," I repeated, though my voice sounded like Chicken Little the first time he declared the sky was falling. "And you just... picked it up and casually tossed it in the fountain?"

He stared at me. I stared back.

"Uh... was I not supposed to?" he asked. "That's what you do, right? With fountains? You toss coins in?"

I swallowed hard. "Well, yeah, usually but... that's the Fountain of Forever."

"I'm guessing there's some Serenade Creek superstition attached?"

I nodded.

"Do you want to tell me what it is?" he asked.

I shook my head.

He took a deep breath and exhaled.

"I never should've said what I said to you earlier," he began, voice soft. Nervous? "Not like that. Not then. Not after everything."

I stayed quiet.

"It probably seemed like it was out of the blue, to you. Like it was just out of nowhere, me saying I wanted something real with you. Like I was using it as a bargaining chip."

I nodded, because it had felt exactly like that.

"What I'm about to say... I'm not going to try to change your mind. I'm not going to try to convince you to give me a chance. Not because I don't want one, but because I never want to be the guy who makes you feel like you can't say no. Your nos matter. What I said... it wasn't out of the blue for me. I'd been thinking about it since the kiss. Well, no. I'd been thinking about it before then, but... telling myself no. I couldn't. Because I didn't want to hurt you."

He ran a hand over his face. "But maybe... I don't know. I think maybe all along I was really most concerned with not getting hurt again myself. I was going to tell you all of this after the wedding."

Something fluttered in my chest. Hope, maybe. Or just relief that I hadn't been completely wrong about him.

"You were?"

"I was," he nodded, shoving his hands in his pockets. "And I was never lying to you, Bailey. I kept saying I couldn't be with you because, well, I'm an idiot."

I laughed behind my hand. Then, lightly, teasingly, I began, "Do you expect me to argue with that because—"

"I might have been lying to myself, though." There was nothing light or teasing in his voice. Or his eyes.

He sat down next to me, his body turned toward mine, our knees almost but not quite touching.

I waited. My heart wasn't beating as much as it was knocking insistently on the door to whatever this was.

Wait. Did I just think that? Ugh. Remind me to never take up poetry.

"Whether we date or not, Bay... Bailey. Whether we date or not? The feelings I have for you are there. I never want you to wonder if they're real."

I shivered, even though it was eighty-five degrees out. With a slight smile, he asked, "Would you like my jacket?"

I nodded. He took it off and put it around my shoulders.

I sucked my bottom lip in between my teeth, gatekeeping the words I wanted to blurt. There were so many of them. This wasn't the time to blurt. It was time to listen. Because I had a feeling... despite everything... deep in my gut... Knox was trying to say everything I'd so badly wanted to hear.

"For so long, I'd shut down love as a possibility, as something that couldn't happen to me again. And maybe I'd let it seem so far away that I hadn't been able to put two and two together—to realize that that was the feeling I had in my chest when I looked at you. When I thought about you. When I heard you laugh."

Chills spread all over my arms and legs.

Did he just say...

Love?

"Knox," I had to interrupt now. I had to. "You don't have to—"

"And yet, I do." He smiled this time—full-fledged, with his mouth and eyes. "Since Stephanie, I thought that the very worst thing you could do to another person was to pretend to love them when you didn't. But maybe. Maybe the opposite is just as bad. To pretend those feelings *aren't* there when they are. Whether we date or not, Bailey Cooper, I've been falling for you since the day we met."

Oh, my stars.

I stared at him, waiting. Because this was the part of the dream where I woke up. Where I always woke up.

"You can say something," he said, gently. "If you want."

"I thought you said you weren't going to try to change my mind? That you wouldn't try to convince me to give you another chance?"

"I wasn't trying to."

"Well, you did," I said, softly.

"I did?" he asked, just as softly.

I nodded.

"I had so many chances—and I blew them."

"You kind of did," I pressed my lips together, but I couldn't fight my own smile. "But uh, you redeemed yourself."

"Bailey Cooper." He took my hands in his. Stroked the back of my knuckles with his fingers. "Will you date me for real?"

We had more to talk about... and we would. We had plenty to work through... and we would. But for now...

"You think love is a possibility for you again?" I asked.

"I think, with you, it's an inevitability," he said. "And I need you to know, I wouldn't say that if I wasn't sure. I'm not going to play with your heart, Bailey Cooper. I'm not going to ever offer you something unless I'm dead set on following through. I can't make promises. But I will follow this through. I will listen to you. I will hear you. And I will always be a safe place for you to say no."

"Yes," I said. And it was the easiest yes I'd ever given, the most heartfelt yes, the yes I said because it was *what I wanted.*

"Yes?"

"Yes. I will date you for real."

"If you need time to think about it—"

"I don't need time to think about it. You got your yes, Showalter," I said, leaning forward, touching my forehead to his.

"I got my yes," he whispered, raising our hands and kissing my knuckles. "The best yes in the history of yeses."

My heart felt like it was on the verge of bursting, but in the best way. I wanted to bottle this moment. To carry it around with me, for all time.

"Can I press my luck and ask one more yes or no question?" he asked.

"If the question is can you kiss me, the answer isn't yes or no. It's if you know what's good for you, you better."

He didn't hesitate. He leaned in and kissed me, his lips slow, reverent, like he was afraid if he moved too fast, I'd run away again. But I wasn't going anywhere.

Not this time.

"Now..." he began, after we broke apart. "Do you want to tell me what I did when I tossed the coin in the Fountain of Forever? Did I bind my soul to the grounds of the Enchanted Rose Inn so that after I die, I won't rest in peace, but I'll haunt the halls of—"

"You told it you were ready for your soul mate."

He raised his brows, and to my surprise, he didn't look at all alarmed. "Oh. Well, okay then."

"Soooo, funny story," I said. "I also accidentally tossed a coin into the Fountain of Forever recently."

"Did you now? How recently?"

"When I first got here," I said. I pointed at the grand entrance of the inn. "And approximately five seconds later, you walked out of that door."

"You're joking."

I shook my head. "No, I am not. I was tossing the nickel to Cherish and it just sort of... went in."

"So... you think it's just another silly Serenade Creek superstition?"

I shrugged. I mean. It had to be, right? And yet...

"Want to know what I think?" he asked.

"Always."

"I think... if you accidentally threw a coin into the Fountain of Forever, telling it you were ready for your soul mate... and five seconds later, I came out of that door?" he paused. "And then... I accidentally threw a coin into the Fountain of Forever right before I confessed my feelings to you?" He brushed my hair behind my ears, his fingers grazing the sides of my face. "I don't think there was anything accidental about it, Bailey Cooper. I think it was the Fountain of Forever, working exactly as it should."

I opened my mouth to agree with him, but before I could say the words... the Fountain of Forever lit up.

"Did you..." his voice trailed off.

He put his arm around me and I rested my head on his shoulder. There were some moments that didn't need words. We both stared at it with wonder, my eyes only straying away when I noticed the first hot air balloon in the sky.

"Look," he whispered, pointing, noticing it at the same time I had.

Cherish always said there were no coincidences in Serenade Creek. And I think she might be right.

Because nothing about this felt like coincidence.

It felt like magic.

For a long time, we didn't say anything, just sat, holding hands, watching the hot air balloon parade.

"I'm going to keep saying yes to what I want," I said. "And work on saying no to what I don't and..."

My voice trailed off as a flash of red swooped by. My cardinal. And then... she flew in. An orangish brown cardinal. A female. She landed right next to the male... on the Fountain of Forever. They tilted their heads toward each other, like they were whispering secrets.

I gasped. "Aww. He found someone."

Knox followed my gaze. "Who?"

"That cardinal." I pointed. "He's been following me around since spring. Everywhere I go."

"That cardinal?" Knox pointed. "The male? Has been following you around since spring?"

"Yeah. And he found his lady."

Knox was quiet a moment.

"I know. I know. You commit and I immediately confess I'm being stalked by a bird. Super normal."

He lifted our hands to his mouth and kissed my knuckles. "Super Serenade Creek," he said. "She's been following me around since spring, by the way."

I turned to him slowly.

"What?" I whispered.

He nodded. "I mean... I don't know that it's the same bird. Obviously. But a female cardinal has been stalking me."

I laughed. "You're kidding."

"100% serious. Everywhere I go. *Purdy purdy purdy.*"

I rested my head on his shoulder again, and he put his arm around me, warm and strong.

"It's the same birds," I said, knowing it with my whole heart. "I think we brought them together."

"Do you now?" he asked.

"I do."

"I have to disagree."

"Oh, do you?" I asked. "Because I have to tell you, Knox, I feel this is an argument I'm going to win."

He leaned in close and whispered, "It's Serenade Creek, Bailey Cooper. I think they brought us together."

Okay. He just might have me there.

"Will you kiss me again, Showalter?"

"If you keep asking questions like that, Cooper, I think I'm going to become the one who can't say no," he said.

CHAPTER TWENTY-TWO

The wedding was perfect.

And it looked like the reception would go off without a hitch as well.

Well... unless you count Greer tripping and falling during our Footloose performance. But she fell right into Corey's waiting arms so... maybe that, too, was more magic than mistake.

Lights strung through the garden like tiny stars that had decided to come down and grant us all their wishes. Jessa was radiant and relaxed. I'd never seen any man look quite as happy as Luke. And me?

Well, I was just enjoying myself because the only person who'd asked me for anything all evening was Knox and his requests were always the same: "May I have this dance?"

He held out his hand again.

But before I could answer, the song faded out and the DJ announced it was time to toss the bouquet.

From where she'd been dancing with Luke, Jessa's eyes zeroed in on me. She shot me a look that practically glowed with mischief.

"I'll just be hiding in the coat closet," I said, standing, and looking around. "If I can find it."

Knox pulled me into a hug, then turned me towards the dance floor. "Go get it, tiger."

I turned back to him, pressing my face into his chest. "I don't want it. Let someone else be the tiger."

He laughed. "You really want to go hide in the coat closet? I'll go with you." He waggled his eyebrows.

"All my single gals... come out, come out wherever you are," Jessa had hopped on the stage and was calling out.

My stomach clenched.

She was holding the Eternal Bouquet.

"Someone really needs to drown that thing in the Fountain of Forever," I muttered.

"All my single ladies... on the dance floor, pleeeeeeeeeeeease!"

"Do I have to?" I asked Knox.

"Of course not," he said. "Not if you don't want to."

I rolled my eyes and groaned. "Well. No one can say I'm cursed anymore, sooo..."

We'd given Jessa her dream wedding. Might as well see it through.

I walked over to stand behind Melody.

Ha ha, I thought. *Come at me now, Eternal Bouquet.*

Melody was just shy of six feet tall and most of her free time was spent playing volleyball. She had this on lock. And if she didn't, there were lots of other girls in front and behind us. A sea of enthusiasm. I'd duck if I had to.

"Here we go!" Jessa called. She turned away from the

crowd, and hurled the bouquet backwards with impressive force.

It sailed over our heads.

Thank goodness.

A gasp went up. I turned with the rest of the crowd, thinking, *Well, at least it wasn't me!*

My eyes widened. My ears burned. I covered my mouth with my hand.

Still standing at our table, way off to the side, a very stunned-looking Knox was holding it.

Noooooooooo.

He caught my eye and burst out laughing.

"Knoxxy, you know what to do!" Jessa called.

"Oh, you bet I do," he called back, but he didn't as much as glance in her direction.

I shook my head as he started towards me, his eyes locked on mine.

The crowd oohed and ahhed, and I said, loud enough for them to hear, "Absolutely not."

Knox just smiled a stupidly handsome smile.

"Get that thing away from me," I said, taking a playful step back as he approached me, shaking it at me.

"It's not cursed this time," he said.

"You don't know that."

"Oh, but I do. Because you don't have to wonder if your guy is gonna show up this time. You don't have to wait. I'm right here. Hand delivery."

A slow chant began. Take *it*, take *it*, take *it*.

"Only if you want to," he said. "Ignore the pressure. Look at me."

He held it out again, his eyes locked on mine.

I looked at the bouquet. Then at him.

"We are the textbook definition of fake it 'til you make it, baby," he said, with a wink.

Did I swoon at his use of the word *baby*? Oh, yeah.

"You're ridiculous," I said.

"You're mine," he whispered back. "And every day, from here on out, I'm going to love you so loud I won't be able to hear the fear."

My breath caught. "You don't have to use the L-word—"

"Yeah. Yeah, I kind of... no, I most definitely do. I love you, Bailey Cooper."

I exhaled. "I might love you loud, too, Knox."

"Then everyone else will just have to wear earplugs."

"So... does this mean you don't hate weddings anymore?"

"I'm a big fan of this one."

He embraced me in front of everyone.

Then he framed my face with his hands, his thumb brushing just beneath my cheekbone, and everything inside me stilled.

And then—*then*—his lips touched mine.

Soft at first. Barely there. Like a question. Like he was giving me time to pull away. To say no.

My eyes welled with tears. Not my usual angry ones, but for the first time in my life that I could recall, happy ones.

I leaned in.

And that was all the answer he needed.

His kiss deepened, slow and sure, the kind that built heat with every breath. His hand slid down to the small of my back, drawing me closer, pressing me against him until there wasn't an inch of space between us. I put my arms around him now because I could. Because I was his... and he was mine. I could hold him anytime I wanted to, a fact I would never take for granted.

It wasn't like the kissing contest kiss—performative and full of nerves and anticipatory grief that it was a one-off. It wasn't like the dance rehearsal kiss, full of longing and swooning.

It wasn't frantic or built on what-ifs and why-nots. It was quiet certainty. It was belonging. It was home.

He kissed like a man who knew he had been given the chance to rewrite every misunderstanding, every hurt, every almost—and he wasn't wasting a single second.

This kiss. This kiss sizzled and there wasn't anything accidental about it. And there was tenderness, too. A quiet reverence that undid me. He kissed me like I was something sacred.

My heart pounded against his chest. His lips lingered on mine, until breathing became optional, until the only thing I could feel was him—his hands, his mouth, his heartbeat thrumming in sync with mine.

With one of his arms wrapped around my waist, with his lips on mine, and the entire crowd cheering for us, even louder than they had at the kissing contest, I took the bouquet from him.

Because maybe it had never been cursed.

Maybe it had known, every time I caught it, that it was my turn.

The timing just had to be right.

And it finally was.

EPILOGUE

"Are you nervous?" Bailey asked.

"Nope. Not at all."

"Well, you're fidgety," she said, poking me in the side.

"I just can't be still around you, my love," I said, leaning over to put my arm around her shoulder, pulling her close for a second, and kissing her temple. Then I admitted, "I might be a little nervous."

Across the room, the Hearts & Charts Brigade went nuts in their booth. Ruby and Cornelia applauded. Stanley gave us a standing ovation. Iris lifted her glass.

Smiling, I raised my sweet tea back at her.

It had been a week since the wedding, and though we weren't the ones who'd gotten married, Bailey and I were definitely solidly in the honeymoon phase of our relationship. We were at the Gather & Grill for Bailey's Friday night dinner with her friends. I had scored an invite, but didn't want to be one of those guys who took their girlfriend away from the other people in her life. Though... yeah, I did want to spend every minute with Bay.

"I don't mind eating alone," I told her. "My usual booth is empty. And I have my book."

I tapped my novel, which sat on the tabletop.

"I know how important these girls' nights are to you. I don't want to be an interloper."

"No way," she said, grinning at me. "The girls can't interrogate you about your intentions if you're sitting all the way over there. Besides, they want you to have dinner with us. Ooh!" she glanced at the door. "Here they are now! And unless I'm hallucinating, Cherish is actually on time?"

I followed her gaze. All four of the women had entered in a cluster, but one headed toward the jukebox, one towards the bathrooms. Cherish just stood there, while the last one, Kelsie, bopped over towards us.

"WHAT IS THIS!" she cried. "I'm gone for a week and when I come back, you have a boyfriend?" Bailey stood up and they hugged like they hadn't seen each other in a couple of months.

"A hot one, too," Kelsie said, giving me a once over. "Get up, Lover Boy. You're part of the family now, and we're huggers."

"Oh, my gosh, Kels." Bailey rolled her eyes, but gestured at me. "Might as well give in. We are huggers and this one does not take no for an answer."

I gave in. There was no resisting the gravitational pull of Bailey Cooper—or her ride-or-dies, apparently.

"Don't squeeze him too tight. I'd like him back in one piece, please."

"Just checking out the biceps, sis. Making sure these arms are strong enough to hold you," Kelsie said to Bailey, after giving me a friendly embrace. Then she leaned in, "I already have a grave dug in my backyard in case you hurt her, mmkay?"

"Kels!" Bailey admonished.

"No, no, if I hurt you, I'd want to be buried in Kelsie's backyard," I told her, giving Kelsie a nod of understanding.

"What is everyone doing?" Bailey asked, settling back in her chair. I pushed it in for her, and then waited until Kelsie was seated to do the same for her.

"Oooh, a gentleman, too," Kelsie said.

These women could eat me alive—or adopt me. I was praying for the latter.

"Why is Cherish hovering by the doorway like she's ready to run?"

Kelsie laughed. "Oh, that. We decided to come over one at a time so as not to overwhelm your gentleman caller."

Bailey scrunched up her nose. "And yet... you got nominated to be the first?"

"I," Kelsie said, pointing back and forth between me and Bailey. "Love this. Love this. I just hate that I missed the kissing contest because I hear that was some kiss."

"I'm sure you can ask, oh, just about anyone in town. I'm sure someone got it on video," Bailey said.

"Or we could just do a reenactment?" I suggested, mostly just to see the tips of Bay's ears turn pink. It's on a very long list of my favorite things about her.

But she surprised me by saying, "Ooh, we could. We could go stand on the family-style table band—"

Kelsie bursted out laughing. "Hey! Come and get him, y'all," she called the others over like she was unleashing a pack of wolves. I took a long sip of sweet tea and braced myself—for interrogation, initiation, or both.

Then Bailey beamed at me and, well, there was no need to brace myself for anything at all. That look could've given me the courage to face an actual pack of wolves.

Bailey patted my forearm. "Prepare yourself."

"Well, well, well," Cherish said, stretching each syllable as far as it would go. "Look what we have here."

Bailey groaned. "Don't start."

"Oh, I will absolutely start. Because I *was right*," Cherish said, sliding into the seat beside Kelsie. "I ushered you right into your happily ever after, girlfriend. I win at life. And I would like my trophy now, thank you very much."

"I'll carve it out of a breadstick," Bailey muttered. But she was smiling.

Cherish winked at me. "You're welcome, Knox."

My lips twitched. "Thank you."

"It's just what I do," Cherish said, gesturing to me and Bailey like we were a museum exhibit. "I change lives. Make dreams come true. Unite hearts and hormones."

"Oh no," Bailey said, smothering a laugh behind her hand. "She's been reading her website testimonials again."

"You joke, but I am extremely good at what I do," Cherish replied, preening as Lyric joined us, giving me a wave and sliding into one of the two remaining empty seats.

"Yeah," Bailey said. "And regardless of the outcome of your shenanigans, I basically saved your business and your butt. I did you a major favor and you owe me a major favor in return and one day, I will collect."

"Way to go, Bay Bay," Lyric said, giving her shoulder a squeeze. "You tell her."

"You hush," Cherish jabbed a finger at Lyric. "Technically, you did a job and were going to be paid well for services rendered, ma'am, if you weren't such a do-gooder."

Bailey rolled her eyes at Cherish. Under the table, she squeezed my knee. Despite the fact that we'd all told her she should, Bailey refused to accept Luke's payment. She told him to consider it a wedding gift.

Addy slid into the seat beside Bailey, her gaze darting toward the door. "I didn't miss anything, did I?"

"Nope," Kelsie said. "Cherish is just soaking up all the credit for being the universe's wingwoman."

Inexplicably, Lyric began singing "The Wind Beneath Your Wings".

Bailey shot me a dry look. "And this is why you don't let them all arrive at once."

I leaned in. "Honestly? I'm kind of enjoying the chaos."

They seemed to be accepting me as easily as my friends had accepted Bay, and could I ask for anything more, really?

Bailey shot me a meaningful look. Now she was the one that was fidgeting—nervous. I gave her a reassuring nod.

She tapped the edge of her glass with her fingernail. "I've got news!"

"We can see your news, darling. All six feet of him are sitting right here," Cherish said, tipping her head toward me with a grin.

"Oh, by the way, Knox," Lyric stopped mid-verse and leaned in with a deadly serious expression. "I'm going to need a list of your favorite songs. I'll cross-reference it with Bailey's and use the overlap to build the foundation for the bespoke playlist I'm curating for you two."

Bailey groaned. "Lyric."

"What?" Lyric said. "Fate needs a soundtrack."

"Could you all please focus for a second?" Bailey asked.

I reached for her hand under the table and gave it a

squeeze. She laced our fingers together like it was the most natural thing in the world.

She straightened up. "Okay. So. I'm going to be gone for most of the summer."

That got their attention.

"Gone where?" Addison asked.

"She and Knox are running away together," Cherish said dramatically.

Bailey laughed. "Well... Kind of."

"Wait, what?" Lyric asked, blinking.

Bailey looked at me, then back at them, eyes shining. "Knox is helping run a summer camp outside Asheville. And he asked me to come with him."

There's no way I could've backed out last minute, but I hadn't wanted to leave Bay for months either. Not after we just got together. I'd made it clear to her, whether we had to be long-distance for a bit or not, I was in this. But she'd been psyched about the idea of coming along.

"No!" Cherish gasped, scandalized. "You're taking her away from us already, you randy scoundrel?"

Addison elbowed her.

"Yes," Bailey said, grinning. "We'll be staying in an actual cabin."

As opposed to a tent the size of a body bag. She'd made sure of that before saying yes.

"There will be crafts and canoes and themed breakfasts," she went on.

"Ugh. That's so disgustingly adorable," Kelsie said. "I love it. But we'll miss you."

"The best part," Bailey said, squeezing my hand. "Knox got me a job. I'm going to be teaching art journaling."

"The pay isn't great, but there are on-the-job perks," I said, winking at Bailey.

"Miss Cooper!" a voice shrieked.

One of our students, Avalynn, was beelining for our table.

"Slow down, Av!" her dad called out.

"Can't!" she hollered, having already reached us. She launched herself into Bailey's lap.

"Whoa!" Bailey caught her with a laugh. "Hi, Avalynn."

"I missed you," Avalynn said, clinging to her neck. "All of the squirrels I paint look like sad potatoes. Hi, Addycakes."

"Hey, sweetheart," Addison said, but she wasn't looking at Avalynn. She was looking at her father, who was walking up to us. "Hi, Evan."

"Hey, Addy," he said. "Everyone."

Avalynn pulled back and looked Bailey dead in the eye. She put her hands on her cheeks. "You're not going to die alone! You're gonna marry Mr. Showalter. Gramma Peach said so!" She turned to me. "Is it true?"

"Ava!" Evan chided. "Didn't we just have a conversation about not asking personal questions?"

Avalynn smacked her forehead lightly. "Ugh. I forgot. So many convos, Dad."

"You do not have to feel obligated to answer anything she asks you, Knox," he said to me.

But all of the women's expectant eyes said otherwise, except for Bailey who was very interested in the ceiling.

I looked at Avalynn, who was staring me down, and said, very seriously, "If I'm the luckiest man in the world, yes, that's exactly how it'll happen."

From all of their reactions, I'd definitely gotten the answer right. But more importantly: I'd answered it honestly.

"You're not going to die alone either," Avalynn matter-of-factly said to Addison. "Because you've got me."

Addy's mouth opened in surprise.

"Come here, you," Evan said, and Bailey helped Avalynn get down. "Let's get out of their hair."

"I'm gonna have chicken nuggies," Avalynn said, straightening her sundress. "You wanna come sit with us, Addycakes?"

"You can if you want to, Addy," Lyric said, quietly. "We won't be offended."

Addy pressed her lips together. Then she shook her head. "No, sweetie. Bailey, uh, Miss Cooper is going away for the summer, so I want to have dinner with her. But next time, okay?"

"You're leaving!" Avalynn cried. "What about my squirrels?"

"I promise I will help you draw squirrels that look like happy potatoes next year," Bailey said, booping the little girl's nose.

I know it's not considered the manliest thing in the world to swoon, but... seeing Bailey's interactions with Avalynn was melting my heart.

"C'mon, kiddo," Evan said. "Have a nice night," he told us.

I couldn't help but notice the way Addy's gaze followed him. The way her smile lingered a little too long. And how Evan, oblivious as most men are, only had eyes for his daughter.

"The best thing is," Bailey began. "I'm going to..."

Her voice trailed off. "Wait," she hauled her purse into

her lap and began rummaging through it. She extracted her phone. "Sorry, this is Wesley. I have to take it."

Addy, Kelsie, and Cherish were exchanging glances. Lyric pushed the breadsticks toward me. "You have to try these. They're delicious," she took one for herself. Then she said, "Wes is Bailey's brother."

"Bailey's hot brother," Cherish said. Lyric handed her a breadstick and she bit off a big bite.

"Thanks, but I know," I said, because Bailey and I had talked about pretty much everything over the past few days, including our families. "I mean, I didn't know he was hot. But uh, good to know, I guess." I finished with a shrug. "But like... Chris Evans hot?"

All four of Bailey's friends burst out laughing.

"Oh, my goodness," Addison said. "You are gonna fit right in."

"Ooh, she went outside," Lyric said. "And she looked upset. Should one of us..."

"I think Knox has got this one," Kelsie said, giving me an encouraging nod.

"I do have this one," I said.

I stood and crossed the restaurant, pushing out into the warm night air.

Bailey was headed towards the bench I'd sat on the last time I was here, and had the phone call from Luke that had... well, oddly enough, lead us right back here.

"Hey," I called.

"I'm okay. I just need a—"

"Bay."

She turned around.

"Angry tears?" I asked, walking towards her, pulling her into a hug.

She shook her head.

Rubbing her back, I asked, "What's up?"

"Wesley's here."

I looked around.

"Not here here, but here in town. He's going to be here for a few weeks and I can't..." she took a deep breath and pulled away so she could look up at me. "I can't leave."

My heart sank.

"Okay," I said.

"I mean... he hasn't lived here in a long time. None of his friends are here anymore. Our mom isn't here anymore. He doesn't really know anyone... except..."

Her frown turned into a slow grin.

"Your girlfriend is a genius, Showalter," she said, and gave me a quick peck on the lips.

"Yes, she is," I agreed, as she extracted herself from my arms. She grabbed my hand and tugged.

"Come on," she said. "Let's go ruin Cherish's life a little. She owes me a favor and I need her to entertain my brother while we're gone."

I chuckled, thinking of Cherish saying Wes was hot. "I go wherever you go, Bailey Cooper."

HEY THERE READER! I hope you loved Bailey and Knox's love story. Ready for your exclusive behind-the-scenes peek at their fling last summer?

Read all about Bailey and Knox's meet cute under the Ferris wheel—and find out how their sparks started flying long before this wedding—when you download *First Kisses and Ferris Wheels, Always a Bridesmaid Prologue.*

Subscribe to Natalie May's Serenade Creek Chronicles and get *First Kisses and Ferris Wheels* FREE! Enter the link down below to find out how to get it...

nataliemayauthor.com/baileyandknoxmeetcute

UP **NEXT IN SERENADE CREEK... Always a Bridesmaid Book 2**

Cherish has mastered the art of being the perfect bridesmaid for everyone else's happily ever after. But when Bailey's brother shows up—and somehow ends up in her orbit—she might just find herself in a relationship... even though she's not looking for love.

Don't miss Cherish & Wes's story in: **Faux Pas and Wedding Gowns, Always a Bridesmaid Book 2**

ABOUT THE AUTHOR

Natalie May writes sweet romantic comedies full of the tropes you love, real feelings, and small towns with way too many opinions. She lives in coastal Florida with her tween son and three rescue cats who may or may not believe they're in charge. When she's not writing love stories with a twist of chaos, she's homeschooling, hiking, or trying (and failing) to finish a cup of coffee while it's still warm.

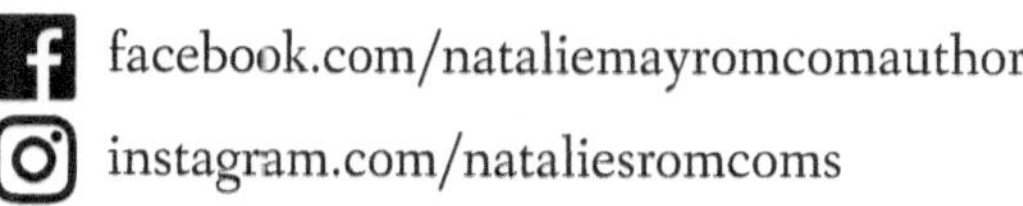